PUFFIN BOOKS

So Far From Skye

Judith O'Neill is an Australian. She grew up in Mildura on the Murray River and studied English literature at Melbourne University. Her own great-great-grandparents were among the crofters who had to emigrate from Skye to Victoria in the 'famine clearances' of 1852. She trained as a teacher in London and has taught in both Australia and Britain. She is married to a fellow Australian and has three daughters. She now lives in Edinburgh. Her earlier books include *Jess and the River Kids*, (shortlisted for The *Young Observer* Teenage Fiction Prize), *Stringybark Summer*, *Deepwater* (shortlisted for the 1989 Children's Book Council of Australia Book of the Year Award for Older Readers) and *The Message*. *So Far From Skye* was shortlisted for the Carnegie Medal, *The Guardian* Children's Fiction Award and in Australia, for the Human Rights Award, where it was highly commended.

D0726608

Another book by Judith O'Neill

HEARING VOICES

Judith O'Neill

So Far From Skye

PUFFIN BOOKS

PUFFIN BOOKS

Published by the Penguin Group
Penguin Books Ltd, 27 Wrights Lane, London W8 5TZ, England
Penguin Books USA Inc., 375 Hudson Street, New York, New York 10014, USA
Penguin Books Australia Ltd, Ringwood, Victoria, Australia
Penguin Books Canada Ltd, 10 Alcorn Avenue, Toronto, Ontario, Canada M4V 3B2
Penguin Books (NZ) Ltd, 182–190 Wairau Road, Auckland 10, New Zealand

Penguin Books Ltd, Registered Offices: Harmondsworth, Middlesex, England

First published by Hamish Hamilton Ltd 1992
Published in Puffin Books 1993
8

Printed in England by Clays Ltd, St Ives plc
Filmset in Bembo

Dedication

This book is dedicated to the memory of my great-great-grand-parents who lived at Hornival near Dunvegan on the Isle of Skye. Donald MacDonald, shepherd and crofter, was born at Talisker; his wife, Effie Campbell, at Borlin. In 1852, they emigrated to Victoria, Australia, with the help of their landlord (MacLeod of MacLeod) and the Highland and Island Emigration Society. They sailed from Liverpool in the *Allison* on the thirteenth of September, 1852, with their five sons, Donald Dubh (my great-grandfather) aged 17, Allan, 14, Donald Bàn, 12, Angus, 8, and William, 4. They landed at Melbourne in December of the same year and went first to work on a sheep-run between Linton and Skipton. Later they settled in Geelong.

Their many descendants remember them with pride.

Author's Note

The voyage of the *Georgiana* from Greenock to Geelong in this story is based on the real voyage of that ship in 1852. The Captain and officers and some of the seamen bear their real names. The Skye families, although imaginary, are drawn from the details of hundreds of families who sailed from Scotland to Australia between 1852 and 1857 with the help of the Highland and Island Emigration Society whose records are kept in the Scottish Record Office, West Register House, Edinburgh. The author would like to thank the staff at the Scottish Record Office, the National Library of Scotland, the Royal Museum of Scotland, and the Merseyside Maritime Museum, Liverpool, for their kind assistance. She would also like to thank Norman Houghton of the Geelong Historical Records Centre, who provided copies of maps and newspapers; Sue and Michael Collins, Donna Hellier and Dorothy Lloyd in Australia, Dr John Bannerman and Margaret Bennett in Scotland, who all gave helpful information or advice; and particularly the Very Reverend Dr James G. Matheson on the Isle of Skye, Dr Donald Meek in Edinburgh, and Catherine O'Neill in London, who generously read the manuscript and made invaluable comments and suggestions.

Some Words

CROFT: A croft is a small piece of land, rented from the landlord by the CROFTER. Crofters also shared grazings with other small tenants in a crofting township.

GAELIC: Pronounced GAL-IK, with the stress on the first syllable. The 'a' may be long as in 'car' or short as in 'Sally'. Gaelic is the Celtic language once spoken widely in the Highlands and Islands of Scotland and still spoken today by a small but determined proportion of the population.

CEILIDH: Pronounced KAY-LEE, with the stress on the first syllable. In the Gaelic-speaking Highlands and Islands of Scotland, a ceilidh is a gathering of friends, neighbours and relations in someone's house to tell traditional tales and sing old songs.

THE FREE CHURCH OF SCOTLAND: The Presbyterian Church that broke away from the Established Church in Scotland at the Disruption of 1843 in protest against the custom of landlords forcing a minister on a congregation against the wishes of the people. Support for the Free Church was almost total in the Highlands and Islands; emigrants took the Free Church with them to Australia and to Canada.

TENANT: A gentleman farmer who rented a large area of land and a fine house from the landlord.

FACTOR: An overseer who managed a property for a landlord in Scotland.

PRECENTOR: A person who led the Psalm singing in the Free Church by singing each line in turn for the congregation to repeat.

CATECHISM: A book for teaching the Christian faith in the form of questions and answers.

Contents

The Isle of Skye: From Talisker to Portree

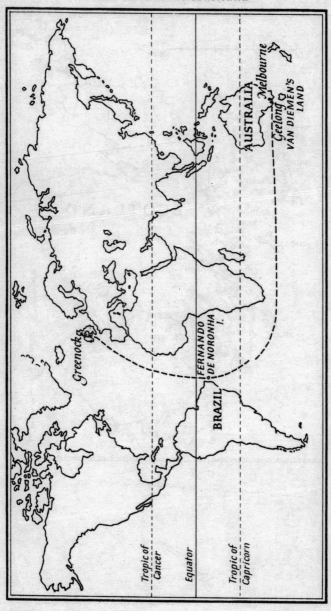

From Scotland to Australia

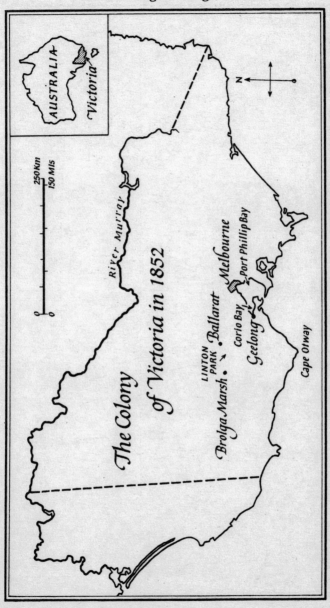

1

Talisker

'Allan, do you really *want* to go to this Colony?'

It was the first time Morag had ever put into blunt words the question she'd been wanting to ask him for weeks, yet she almost guessed the answer before he gave it.

'No! Of course I don't!' Her brother's voice was indignant. 'But it's not a matter of whether I *want* to go. We've got no choice. We *have* to go! And so do the MacKinnons and the Mathesons and all of us here at Talisker!'

Morag sighed. She knew he was right. They had to go.

She was standing with Allan in the late afternoon near the top of the waterfall and looking down for the last time into Talisker Bay. They saw the sharp grey rock at the Point, the white-fringed curve of the sea, the yellow sand where they'd searched for shellfish in the famine years, and the green marshy land running back to the big house, Talisker itself, in its nest of trees. Far below they could see the tiny figure of a woman. Even on this very last day, Janet Matheson was still gathering seaweed. Morag watched as the old woman bent to pick up each leathery strip from the sand and tossed it over her shoulder into the creel on her back.

'Why's she still collecting all that seaware, Morag?' asked Allan. He was well over fourteen and taller than his sister who was only a year younger. They looked strikingly alike with their dark untidy hair and the same brown eyes as their mother. 'There'll be no one left here to spread it on the earth or to dig it in. Why does she bother?'

'Just habit,' said Morag. 'Janet's always been the one to bring in the seaweed for the crofts so I suppose she likes to keep doing it till the last minute. Perhaps it helps her forget we're all leaving tomorrow.'

Morag glanced up at Allan. Her eyes went from his broad face to his thin legs. She stared down at his bare feet on the heather.

'Do you know what Janet told me about the Colony last night?' she asked him. 'She says the people out there have their feet turned round the wrong way. They have the heels in front and the toes at the back.'

Allan laughed.

'Janet Matheson's full of old stories, Morag. There's not a word of truth in most of them. That can't be true about the feet.'

'Perhaps everyone walks backwards there,' said Morag, still puzzled. 'The Colony *is* on the other side of the world you know.'

'No, they don't walk backwards! Everyone walks just the way we walk here. Mr Chant told Father it's a lovely country. Exactly like our own Isle of Skye but much warmer and not nearly so misty or wet.'

'I know that,' said Morag. 'Father's told me a hundred times. And there's plenty of work for everyone and there's no potato blight and no cholera either. But what I don't know is if it's near the sea.'

'Of course it's near the sea! Australia's an island too! Just like Skye! Island people need the sea. They're sure to know that in the Colony.'

Morag thought Allan didn't sound quite as certain of himself as usual. He was blustering on and on and waving his skinny arms about. It struck her that he didn't really know much more about the Colony of Victoria than she did. But he was right about one thing. They all had to go there. And the families from their own little township at Talisker weren't the only ones. Hundreds of other poor crofters were leaving Skye this year. Whole shiploads of them. Their landlords were even paying part of the fare to be rid of them and the Emigration Society was lending the rest. Morag's father always said angrily that the landlords were clearing the people off the land to make room for their new flocks of sheep, but Mr Chant, the emigration man, said it was just because there were too many people on the Island and not enough work or food to keep them. Whatever the real reason, Morag knew the crofters were being 'put away'. That's what everyone kept saying.

'Why don't we just refuse to go, Allan?' she asked him.

'Someone's tried that over on the mainland. It didn't work. The landlord sent his factor along and he said, "Either you set off for the ship today or we'll burn your house to the ground." So they packed up their things and walked straight to the ship.'

'But *our* landlord here on Skye wouldn't ever do that to us, Allan! The MacLeod's a good man. Look how he helped us with bags of oats through the famine years. He went bankrupt trying to feed us. He's not like those other land-lords.'

'Well, maybe he wouldn't actually turn us out,' Allan admitted. 'But there's always that fear in people's minds. And there's the fear of the blight coming back again to kill off the potatoes. No one wants to go through those terrible hungry years again. You haven't forgotten what it was like, have you?'

Morag hadn't forgotten. The green potato plants had turned black overnight and the families on Skye had had nothing to eat but shellfish from the rocks and an occasional bag of oats. She still remembered the stink of those rotting plants. And after the famine had come the cholera. She shivered.

'If we stay here,' Allan went on, 'things can only get

3

worse. The more of those peculiar new sheep they bring in from the south, the less land there'll be for the crofters and their families. And anyway, the landlords say they don't need so many shepherds now, even though their flocks are bigger. If we want to eat, we've got to go.'

Morag turned away from Talisker Bay and looked inland, up towards the glen. In the far distance she saw the Black Cuillins, blue not black in the summer light, those extraordinary mountains at the heart of the Isle of Skye. Closer at hand she saw the cluster of five low stone huts near the river – the little township of Talisker. The huts were roughly thatched with heather and turf, each roof held down with heavy stones that hung from ropes around the eaves. The ropes criss-crossed the thatch like a net. Beside each hut stood a peat-stack, carefully cut and piled up for a winter that the people would never see. To Morag's eye, those squat black houses and peat-stacks looked strangely alike. On a dark night you could hardly tell one from the other. More than once she'd blundered around the peat-stack, trying to find a door that wasn't there.

She watched a small crowd of women and children leading five shaggy Highland cows in through the back gate of the big house. Each cow was held by a grass rope tied to her wide-branching horns.

'It was kind of Talisker to buy the cows,' said Morag. 'Look! There they go now!' Talisker was the man and Talisker was the house. His sheep lived off the Mac-Leod's good land on this western edge of Skye near the sea.

'Kind!' snorted Allan. 'He didn't pay us much, Morag. We didn't get the proper price. He knew we had to sell. We can't take our Peggy to the Colony!'

'I wish we *could* take her,' said Morag sadly. 'Peggy's lived in the house with us for four winters now and she's never been any trouble. I've taken her up to the grassy shieling on the hills for three summers too. She'll be sad

4

tonight, cooped up with a lot of strange cows in Talisker's byre.'

'Mother's the one who'll be sad and crying tonight,' said Allan. Morag had never heard his voice so bitter. 'It's not just her cow she's losing. There are her hens too. Talisker's bought the lot.'

'But we're taking Skerry with us!'

'Of course Skerry'll go with us. You can't part a shepherd from his dog. There'll be big landlords out in the Colony, just the same as here. They're sure to need good shepherds like Father to look after their sheep – and good dogs like Skerry too.'

'But Allan, will *all* the shepherds be allowed to take their dogs? There could be a hundred dogs on the ship. Whatever will they eat?'

Allan exploded. 'You're always asking these questions, Morag!' he said. 'I don't know all the answers, do I?'

Morag just laughed. She knew it was true but she couldn't stop herself.

'I've still got one more,' she said. 'It's about the English. The language I mean. Will we have to learn it? Mother says the people out in the Colony don't all have the Gaelic. Could that be true, do you think?'

Allan's irritation had gone at once. This was one question he was glad to answer.

'It could be true,' he said. 'But you don't need to worry, Morag. You know very well that Father has a bit of the English and I have six or seven words of it. I picked them up at the market when he took me droving with him last year. That should see us through.'

Allan seemed very pleased with himself all of a sudden.

'But what about me?' insisted Morag. 'And what about Mother and little Flora and Kenny? Will we all have to learn the English?'

'I don't know. But I told you. I have six or seven words already. That'll be a start. I can easily teach you.'

'We won't get far on six or seven words!' said Morag. She swung around suddenly to face the open sea. 'Look Allan! You can see the other islands so clearly today.' She gazed out across the water at three distant blue humps against the skyline – South Uist and Barra with tiny Eriskay between them. 'Will the people over there be going to the Colony too?'

'Next year, probably. Our ship's full of Skye families but bit by bit the landlords'll be clearing the other islands too. One day we might even meet someone from South Uist or Barra out in the Colony. But I don't think we'd really want to be meeting them, Morag. We'd do better just to stick to the Skye folk.'

A great sea-eagle soared in slow circles far above their heads. Its white tail-feathers were gleaming in the sunshine and the enormous wings were stretched out to their fullest span. Morag and Allan tipped back their heads and watched the magnificent bird as it glided effortlessly over Talisker Bay and off towards another waterfall that hurtled over the cliff's edge further south. The spray of that waterfall flew high into the air, blown up by the wind off the sea. A tall white waterfall spouting into the sky! As Morag watched, the distant eagle plummeted to earth.

'We'd better go home,' she said sadly.

Morag and Allan hurtled down the steep path from the cliff. They reached the drove-road from Fiskavaig and crossed the rocking planks of a bridge over the river. Near the back gate of Talisker, they turned into the glen and soon they were standing among the five black houses. Close to the river and up the sides of the hill lay the crofts themselves, those beloved patches of land where the five families had grown their rows of potatoes till the years of the blight. Now the plants were beginning to sprout again but they still looked unhealthy and the lazy-beds were choked with nettles. Piles of seaweed lay rotting by the river. The place seemed half-dead already.

That night, as Morag lay beside little Flora on a heap of heather in one corner of the dark hut, everything seemed strangely quiet without their hens clucking and flapping on the shiny black rafters. In the faint light from a smoky peat fire burning on the hearth in the centre of the room, Morag could just make out the shapes of Allan and young Kenny on their mattress of dried grass near the door. She could hear her mother and father talking anxiously to each other in the bed by the wall. She wished she could get to sleep but the summer night was so short. Midnight had passed before the last light of evening had faded from the doorway and soon after three o'clock the first light of morning shone in. Everyone in the black house was restless, waiting for the early start. Morag heard her mother crying in the brief darkness.

The whole family was up and dressed before five. Mother dished the porridge onto their plates and they walked up and down outside in the cold bright sunshine to eat it, scraping up the thick salty mush with their fingers. Then they followed Father back into the house. He snatched his cap off his head, wiped his hands against his trousers, and took the Bible carefully down from the shelf. He opened it up to make sure Grandfather's Waterloo medal was still tucked safely between the pages. Then he wrapped the Good Book in a piece of blanket and folded it into the very centre of a bundle of clothes. He tied the bundle with rope.

Mother packed her last few things – a white milk-jug and a long black skirt – into a wooden box. She poured a dish of water over the fire and the whole family stood and watched in silence as the glowing peat hissed and spat and the last flame died. The water soaked into the mud of the floor. Father stooped under the doorway and led the way out of the hut. He was a tall man and broad-shouldered, with thick red hair and beard. Mother came next, small

7

and dark-haired. She wore her white mutch on her head. Then Flora and Kenny. Morag and Allan came last.

'I'm taking the foot-plough, Effie!' Father said suddenly, unhooking the awkward thing from the outside wall. 'How can we grow potatoes out there if we can't dig the soil?'

'It's very heavy to carry, Donald,' said Mother, 'and Mr Chant told us there'd be no need for foot-ploughs in the Colony. He says they use some other kind.' She tied the porridge-pot onto the smallest bundle and put it into Kenny's arms.

'I know he said that but I'm taking it all the same! If they won't let me bring it on board, I'll give it to someone in Portree. I'm not leaving my plough here for Talisker to burn to ashes when we've gone!'

'Here's the cart!' shouted Kenny. 'Everyone's ready! Come on! Come on!' Kenny was the youngest and the only one in the family to think there was something exciting about this terrible day. Even Flora, who was only nine, understood it was no day for laughing or smiling. She kept her pale face very serious as she watched the other four families hurrying out of their huts, clutching their few belongings in their arms. The MacKinnons, the Mathesons, the MacAskills and the MacInneses. Flora had even let her mother pour a cup of cold river-water over her hair to make it sit in place, just for this one day. Kenny had absolutely refused to have any water on his head. He laughed out loud now as he ran towards the cart.

Talisker was lending his own cart and horse for their journey over the Island. He was up early himself. A smooth, well-dressed man, plump and smiling, he stood just inside his back gate, looking out through the bars at the five families as they loaded up their bundles and boxes. Janet Matheson climbed nimbly on top of the pile, her torn skirt hitched high above her dirty bare feet. A black shawl covered her neat cap and white hair. Her old face was wrinkled and brown. Morag couldn't help thinking it was

8

a wonder Janet was allowed to go to the Colony at all. She wasn't going to be much use out there, except for picking up bits of seaware, but the Mathesons had refused to leave Skye without her or without Alec, her husband, so there she was, perched on the bundles of bedding and clothes and shouting down instructions to everyone else. Morag liked Janet. She was old and bossy but there was something about her that made Morag feel a bit more comfortable on this last bleak morning.

'Pass me up the baby, Rachel!' Janet called to her daughter-in-law. 'Your arms'll drop off if you carry him the whole way. I'll make him a little bed up here. He'll be sleeping like an angel all day long.'

Rachel Matheson passed up the baby, tightly wrapped in a square of bleached cloth. Then the MacKinnon baby went up too, kicking and squealing, and the skinny, silent MacInnes baby. Janet arranged them all in soft furrows among the bundles.

Talisker opened his gate. He came right out and went to shake hands with the men. They hesitated for an instant but then Morag's father, Donald MacDonald, stepped slowly forward and took the outstretched hand. The other crofters followed him, one by one. They shook Talisker's hand but no one spoke a word and no one looked the man in the eye. To the crofters' way of thinking, tenants like Talisker, in their fine big houses, were no better than the landlords in their castles. All of them, landlords and tenants, wanted the same thing. They wanted the people cleared off the land. As soon as the stiff farewells were over, Talisker retreated behind his gate again, a smile on his handsome face. He was glad they were going.

Now came the moment Morag had been dreading. They were leaving the black houses. They were leaving the township of Talisker. They were leaving the Isle of Skye. She bent down to pick up an empty white shell from the scattering that lay by the hut and she slid it into her pocket.

Her mother ran back to put a hand just one more time on the smooth grinding-stones outside the door. Her father scooped up a handful of black earth and poured it into the pouch that hung from his waist. Then they were off.

Talisker's new shepherd led the horse. He was a lowlander and spoke not one word of the Gaelic. None of the crofters wanted to talk to him so it didn't matter that few of them could understand his strange Scots tongue. He'd come to Skye from the south only a few months back, along with the new flocks of sheep. Behind the horse and the loaded cart trudged the five families. Most of them walked barefoot though some had a pair of black boots strung around their necks. There was no need for boots in summer. The soles of their feet were tough and hard.

The crofters' drab clothes were torn and ragged but much cleaner than usual. There'd been two big wash-days by the river early in the week. The women had trodden every stitch of clothing and every piece of blanket in the tubs and had spread them out on the heather to dry. The younger children walked close to their mothers. The smallest of them tottered along on spindly legs. Morag knew that before long some of these little ones would have to be carried. They'd never manage to walk right across the Island in two days. She watched Kenny. He was still cheerful and almost skipping. Although he was thin like all the others, he seemed healthy enough under his wild thatch of hair, almost as red as Flora's and their father's. Kenny was quite tough for a boy of seven but some of the other children still had stomachs swollen from the years of hunger. Morag's eyes moved to her mother. Effie MacDonald walked near Mary MacAskill who was expecting her sixth child in two months' time. Mary moved heavily, a grizzling three-year-old pulling on her hand.

Behind the women and the younger children came Morag herself with Allan and Flora and all their cousins and friends. Last of all walked the men, two of them with massive foot-ploughs like Donald's hoisted up against the plaids on their shoulders, and others with their long shepherd's crooks in their hands. Neil MacKinnon had his pipes tucked under one arm. Old Alec Matheson limped badly, an awkward bundle stuffed under his coat, but somehow he managed to keep up with the others. The sheepdogs ran beside the men, their tails drooping, as if even they knew what was happening. The people walked in silence, looking back now and then at the huts by the river and at Talisker himself, still watching them from behind his barred gate. This sad summer morning was brilliant with sunshine. The sky was cloudless and blue. The Cuillins stood out sharp and clear and the skylarks were singing high above the heather. Morag didn't know if the fine weather made the leaving better or worse. She almost wished the rain would fall and the sky turn black. That would have blended better with the feelings inside her.

The track followed the bends of the Talisker River for the first mile or so. As soon as the straggling procession had rounded the curve of a hill, so that when the crofters looked back they could no longer see their township, then the wailing began. Janet Matheson started it, perched on the cart with the babies and the bundles. She let out a long desperate cry of grief and the other women took it up. The men joined in and then the children. A few of the women shed real tears but for the most part the crying was dry-eyed. It rose and fell like a wild song of death, like a terrible funeral lament, as the bare feet tramped or limped or dragged their way along the track to Carbost. Only the stolid lowland shepherd and the three sleeping babies took no part at all in the keening and crying.

At Carbost, on the edge of sparkling Loch Harport, three more families were waiting to join them. One woman was clutching her spinning-wheel and no one could persuade her to leave it behind.

'It was my mother's!' she insisted, 'and her mother's before her. I can't live without it!'

Janet Matheson helped her find a safe place for the spinning-wheel right at the back of the cart. More bundles and boxes were packed around it.

Now Mr Cameron, the minister, came hurrying out from his small white manse by the Free Church. His wife was beside him. They greeted the travellers from Talisker and seized every hand in turn. This was the moment when the tears really did begin to flow. The minister was their friend and he knew every one of them, even the smallest children. He'd stuck by them through the famine years and he'd made sure they were given their bags of oats when the potato plants had shrivelled, but there was nothing at all he could do to stop this tide of emigration. He tried to tell them now that things would be better for them in the Colony, that the flitting from Skye would prove a blessing and not a curse, that their children would find a happier life there.

'The Colony will be like the Promised Land for you,' he said, his voice breaking. 'A wonderful land, flowing with milk and honey.'

But no one believed him and he hardly seemed to believe it himself. He was a Skye man, after all. He knew that the crofting families couldn't bear to be moved from this Island where they'd been born. So he suddenly stopped trying to tell them it was all for the best and he let himself cry with them.

'Allan,' said Mr Cameron, brushing away his tears on the sleeve of his black coat and seizing Allan's arm. His voice was steady now. 'You and Morag are good scholars even though you've hardly ever managed to come all the way to our little school here in Carbost. Neil MacKinnon's done a grand job teaching you all he knows in the township every winter. You two read the Gaelic better now than anyone else from Talisker and you write it better too. Far better than your father, though he wouldn't like me to say it. So I want to hear from you both, remember. A letter from every port – if there are any ports – and a long letter from the Colony when you get there. The few families that are left hereabouts will be waiting for your news. So put it all in. Even the sad things that happen and the good things too.'

'I don't think there'll be any good things, Mr Cameron,' said Allan. 'And anyway, we've got no paper. No paper at all and no pencil or pen. So how can we write?' He spoke politely enough but he didn't sound very keen on the idea of writing letters.

'We'd be glad to write if we had the paper, Mr Cameron,' said Morag quickly, trying to cover up Allan's abruptness.

'I'll give you some!' cried the minister at once. 'This very minute.' And he almost ran back to his house and came out again with a sheaf of his own fine sermon paper and two sharp new pencils.

'That'll do you to start with,' he said, pushing the paper and the pencils into Morag's hands. 'You might find pens and ink on the ship. Just ask for them! Ask the Captain himself for a wee bottle of ink!'

Morag smiled up at him.

'Have you ever been on one of those big ships, Mr Cameron? Ships like the *Georgiana*?'

The minister shook his head.

'Never,' he said. 'I've only been on the little Islands' ship, Morag. Years ago when I was a student in Glasgow and a few times since.'

'I think the big ships are different, Mr Cameron,' said Morag. 'I don't think you can talk like that to the Captain on one of those big ships. I don't think you can talk to him at all. I wouldn't like to ask him for a wee bottle of ink.'

The minister looked disappointed.

'You could be right, Morag. The *Georgiana* won't be quite the same as the little Islands' ship, will it? Not so friendly. But there's sure to be *someone* you can ask. I don't believe there'd be a ship full of Skye crofters and not a single bottle of ink amongst them. Just keep on asking. Don't sit and wait for things to happen. Make them happen yourself. Remember that, Morag, and you too, Allan.'

They nodded. Mr Cameron had one last word for them.

'Now don't forget to be praying to the good Lord every day!' he said, tears springing in his eyes again.

'We won't forget, Mr Cameron,' said Allan. 'And we won't forget you.'

'May the Lord Himself go with you!' said the minister, turning quickly away.

The final farewells were said and the travellers set off again. The wailing cry rose up once more. Alec Matheson complained that his legs were tired. He clambered onto the cart to sit beside his Janet.

'What's in that white bundle under his coat?' Allan whispered to Morag. 'Look, he's hiding it in the pile of bedding.'

'I think it's his fiddle,' Morag whispered back.

'Lucky the minister didn't see it,' laughed Allan quietly. 'He's never liked those old songs and dances that Alec Matheson plays at the weddings and the ceilidhs. He might've made him throw the fiddle away.'

Morag was silent and puzzled. She knew what the minister thought about Alec's fiddle. He didn't like Janet's old stories either. But Morag loved those stories about the little quiet people who live underground and about the witches and the water-horses. Whenever the Talisker families had gathered around the fire in the ceilidh-house, it was Janet Matheson who always had the best tales to tell. Mr Cameron had never managed to stop them and he hadn't stopped Alec's songs either.

'Why doesn't he like them, Allan?' she asked at last. 'He's

a good man, isn't he? He's always helped us. What's he got against our old songs and stories?'

'He thinks God doesn't like them,' muttered Allan, 'but he must be wrong about that.'

'Allan!' boomed their father's voice, close behind them. 'Who's that you're saying is wrong?'

'The minister, Father.' Allan's face was flushed with embarrassment.

'The minister! Wrong!' cried Father sharply. 'Don't you ever let me hear you saying such a terrible thing again! The minister's the Man of God! He's never wrong! Remember that!'

'Yes, Father,' said Allan, trying to sound meeker than he felt.

But Morag thought her own thoughts to herself. Thoughts about Alec Matheson's fiddle and the old songs. Thoughts about Janet Matheson's stories and the wonderful tales her grandmother from Borlin used to tell her years ago. She wasn't ever going to forget them. They belonged to the Isle of Skye. She knew those songs and stories were safe inside her head. She was taking them with her to the Colony, like the small white shell in the pocket of her dress.

2

Portree

'Ferry!' shouted a voice from the edge of the loch. 'Free
crossings today!'

Everyone stopped to look. The ferryman's boat was so
small that only a few of the travellers could possibly accept
his offer to take them across Loch Harport.

'Let Mary MacAskill go and one of the other women
with a few of the little children,' said Morag's father. 'That'll
shorten the walk for them by about four miles. The rest of
us can keep on around the head of the loch.'

Two mothers and five tired children hurried down to
the boat, delighted to rest their legs.

'We'll wait for you on the other side!' Mary MacAskill
called as she climbed awkwardly into the boat.

The ferryman pulled on his oars and sang mournfully as
the boat moved out across the water. Morag was glad to
be still walking steadily on with the rest. She didn't want
to let that cart out of her sight even for an hour. Who
knows, she thought to herself, what that lowland shepherd
might get up to if they didn't keep an eye on him? He'd
be rifling through their bundles perhaps, to see what he
could find. He might even take Grandfather's medal with
its faded ribbon! They tramped on round the head of the
loch and then doubled back towards Bracadale, meeting
up with the ferry folk halfway along the shore.

At the end of the day, their pace slowing as the children

grew weary, the crofters came to Bracadale with its wide loch, open to the sea and dotted with tiny green islands. Bracadale township looked a miserable place to Morag. It was nothing more than a collection of dilapidated black houses on the bare hillside and the air was heavy with the smell of rotting seaweed. But the door of every hut stood open to welcome them. There were more cousins here and more cousins of cousins, waiting eagerly to draw them inside and to give them food and to put them to bed on bundles of grass on the floor.

In the early morning, a still larger group of crofters moved off towards Portree. Ten more families from Bracadale had joined them and only a few of the elderly folk and a couple of shepherds were left behind. At the very last minute one family suddenly refused to go, taking their bundles off the cart and turning away in tears.

A mile beyond Bracadale, Morag caught her foot on a stone and fell heavily to the ground, twisting her ankle and crying out with the pain. Her father hoisted her up to ride the last part of the journey on the cart, along with Alec and Janet Matheson and the babies. She held on tight to the MacInnes baby to stop him from rolling off and she listened to Alec who was singing away to himself as the wheels bumped beneath them. It was one of the old journeying songs he was singing. Morag had heard it often enough in the ceilidh-house when all the Talisker families had sat around the fire to listen. She sang it with him now but not so loudly that her father could hear. Donald MacDonald wouldn't mind the first verse or even the last verse. The middle verses were the ones he wouldn't like. Morag wondered again how a kind man like her father could be so fierce about those harmless old songs and stories. She kept her voice low. No one could hear her at all except Janet and Alec Matheson, riding there beside her on the cart.

May the good God be with us wherever we go,
Over the green hills and over the sea,
Far from the Island, so far from our home,
Over the green hills and over the sea.

May the red sun be with us wherever we go,
Over the green hills and over the sea,
Waking us early, so far from our home,
Over the green hills and over the sea.

May the new moon be with us wherever we go,
Over the green hills and over the sea,
Silver and shining, so far from our home,
Over the green hills and over the sea.

May the fairies be with us wherever we go,
Over the green hills and over the sea,
Bringing us blessing, so far from our home,
Over the green hills and over the sea.

May the angels be with us wherever we go,
Over the green hills and over the sea,
Watching and keeping us, far from our home,
Over the green hills and over the sea.

'Stop!'

A sudden cry rang out in front of the cart. The horse shied and pulled up abruptly. Morag clapped a hand over her mouth and stopped her singing. The dishevelled figure of a woman had run out from an abandoned gravel pit beside the track. Her black hair, uncovered by cap or shawl, hung right down her back. Her face was smeared with mud and looked strangely old. She had no proper clothes on at all but just a worn-out blanket wrapped tight around her shoulders. It hid most of her body from neck to ankles but there were gaps here and there where patches of dirty, bare skin showed through. She was waving her arms up and down in front of the startled horse. Two sharp-faced boys and a girl crept out of the gravel pit behind her. Their pieces of blanket were far more skimpy than hers. They stared at all the people with round, frightened eyes and the people stared back.

'It's a witch!' screamed Kenny and ran sobbing to his mother.

'Don't be silly, son,' said his mother but even she looked alarmed as she watched the woman pulling those three thin children towards the cart.

'We're going too!' shouted the woman, her voice rough and hoarse. 'The man said we could go on the ship. He told us to be ready. Don't leave us behind!'

'But where's your husband?' asked Morag's father gently. He came forward and peered down into the gravel pit.

'Dead!' said the woman flatly. 'Died in the famine. No use looking in there for him.'

'Where do you live then?' he asked, gazing around him. There wasn't a hut in sight.

'Down in that gravel pit.' She jerked one arm and pointed. 'We rigged up a sail and we piled up the heather. That kept off the rain. Two years we've been there.'

'But what do you eat?'

'Folk give us this and that. Folk round here are kind, you know. Skye families are never mean.'

Morag thought the two boys looked as if they could have eaten a great deal more. Their filthy legs were like sticks. The girl was no better.

'And Mr Chant said you could go to the Colony?' Donald MacDonald could hardly believe it and Morag understood why. What use would these half-starved pit-children be when they got there? The Colony was supposed to need big, strong men.

'He told me the boys could work with the sheep,' said the woman. 'And he said I could cook for the shepherds. I *can* cook, you know!'

She glared defiantly at Morag's father. She held out a

scrap of paper for him to see. He read it slowly, one finger following the Gaelic words, his lips moving. He passed the paper up to Morag and asked her to read it too. She leant down from the cart and murmured the words to him. At last he nodded and he smiled at the woman.

'Of course you can walk along with the rest of us, Mistress Gordon. I often used to meet your husband at the market in the years before the famine. Your ship's the same as ours. The *Georgiana* from Greenock on the 13th July, 1852 – it's written here on your paper right enough. So we'll all stick together. My son'll keep an eye on your children for you. Allan, where are you?'

Allan stepped forward, none too pleased that Morag had been called on to help with the reading. He didn't seem very enthusiastic as he looked at the two dirty boys and the girl, crouching behind their mother. The girl was coughing. She bent over as the cough rasped through her lungs.

'These are the Gordon boys,' said Father. 'Ewen and Calum. And this is their sister, Kirsty. They'll go with you, Allan. Slow down to their pace now. They don't look as if they could hurry.'

The wild mother joined the walkers. All the fight in her had melted away.

'They're good children,' she said quietly to Morag's mother.

The good children hobbled along the track, the two boys on one side of Allan, the girl on the other. They looked scared as if they were afraid he might lift a hand suddenly and hit them. Morag watched them from her perch on the cart.

'Allan won't hurt you,' she called down to them.

The three looked up at her, surprised. The older boy smiled. That must be Ewen, she thought, and smiled back at him. He seemed to be about Allan's age. Kirsty waved a small, bony hand but then bent over again, seized by a new fit of coughing. Morag liked the look of the gravel-pit family in spite of the dirt and the holey blankets and the girl's terrible cough.

There was no more singing now from Alec Matheson as the families walked on. Just the creak of the cartwheels and the heavy plod of the horse and the soft sound of so many bare feet going down the long track to Portree.

'There are the ships!' shouted Morag. She was the first to catch sight of the forest of tall masts and sails in the harbour. Among the fishermen's boats were two fine paddle-steamers with raked funnels, tied up side by side at the jetty.

'Don't you be bothering with those steamships, girl,' hissed Janet Matheson in her ear. 'We'll be reaching them all too soon. Look behind you at the hills. That's the sight you'll be wanting to remember!'

Janet herself had turned her back on Portree and on the two steamers in the harbour. She pulled her black shawl still tighter around her head and gazed steadily at the Cuillins as if to fix their razor-sharp peaks and ridges in her mind forever. Morag did the same for a minute or two but then the fascinating tug of the tall masts and red funnels drew her eyes back to the sea.

'Those two paddle-steamers are far too small to go all the way round the world,' she said. 'We'll all be drowned! I thought we were going on a big ship!'

'They're not taking us all the way round the world, Morag,' laughed Alec Matheson, dragging his fiddle out of hiding now and clutching it in his arms like a baby. 'Those are just the little West Highland steamers. They'll take us down the coast to Greenock. That's where you'll see the big ship. The *Georgiana*. More's the pity!'

Portree was seething with people. Families were arriving wearily on foot from Duntulm and Uig in the north, from Husabost and Dunvegan in the west, from Kilmore and Caradal in the south. Whole boatloads from even more distant parts of Skye were sailing into the blue harbour and disembarking at the jetty. All of them had the same drawn faces and the same bundles of possessions in their arms. Sheepdogs were barking. Babies were crying. Friends and relations who hadn't met since the last funeral were greeting each other with tears.

'We must all keep together!' shouted Donald Mac-Donald to his little flock. 'We'll unload the cart now and send it back to Talisker. Find your own things and keep a tight grip on them. And don't wander away from the rest of us or we'll never end up on the same steamer to Greenock.'

The families pressed in close beside him. Morag had climbed down from the cart and she stood on one leg, easing the weight off her sore ankle. She passed the squalling MacInnes baby back to his mother and grabbed her bundle as Allan hoisted the wooden box high on his shoulder. Now the whole crowd was surging forward towards the ships. Right by the side of the jetty, almost at the water's edge, sat a man behind a table, the Emigrant Book open before him.

'No one can go on board without the paper!' this official called out as the people pushed closer. 'Present yourself family by family. No shoving there! And no dogs!'

'No dogs?' The cry of anguish and disbelief went up from every mouth.

'No dogs!' repeated the man.

All the shepherds joined in the shouts of protest and anger. How could they look after sheep in the Colony if they had no dogs? The dogs were part of their families. They'd almost sooner leave their children behind than leave their dogs!

But their shouting did no good at all. The man was firm. No dogs were to be taken on board.

'Get rid of them somehow!' he shouted. 'And be quick about it.'

Morag knew that as long as she lived she'd never forget the next terrible hour as the families parted from their dogs. Grown men were crying in the street.

'What'll become of our Skerry?' she asked her father.

'Just stay here, all of you,' he said, his voice choked and thick. 'Let the men come with me and bring the dogs. I've got a cousin here in Portree. Black Duncan. He'll mind them for us. Come on.'

'First they take our land and then they take our dogs!' bellowed Neil MacKinnon, holding on fiercely to the little white dog he'd had for nine years.

'Come on, man,' said Donald MacDonald, 'and we'll find my cousin.'

'He never could feed so many!' protested Neil.

'He can feed them for a day or two. Then he'll find them new homes. Come on! Hurry! Or those steamers'll be off without us.'

Every crofter made for the house of a cousin or a friend. Some cousins were landed with five dogs or more but they promised to do their best for them. No one would let a good sheepdog starve. A few of the shepherds simply led their dogs out to the road and pointed their noses back in the direction from which they'd come.

'Go home, Finn!' cried one of them.

'Home, Corrie!' ordered another.

Obediently the dogs ran off, never looking behind them, running for miles over the Island. They knew their way home. The folk left in the townships would be sure to look after them. The men trailed back to their families. Not one of them seemed the same without that familiar dog at his heels.

'Hurry up, now!' called the man at the table. 'Family by family. And have your papers ready.'

It was a long, slow business getting all those bewildered people on board. Donald MacDonald kept his group together. Mistress Gordon with her boys and Kirsty never left his side. They showed their papers in turn, their names were ticked off on the list, they walked up the narrow gangplank of the *Duntroon Castle*. There were no bunks or cabins. Just the open deck with crofters lined up close together, family by family, their bundles between them. More and more people were crammed on board till Morag began to be afraid they'd sink to the bottom of the harbour under such a weight. They were packed in like beasts going to market. The Highland sailors gave out chunks of black bread and buckets of fresh water. That was meant to last them for the day and a half it might take to steam down to Greenock but no one felt like eating yet. Everyone sat huddled on the deck, stunned into silence by the grief of leaving the Isle of Skye. The man with the Emigration Book came on board last.

It was late now, well after ten at night. The sun had set but the sky was only just beginning to darken. The tide was on the turn. The Captain shouted his orders. The crew stood ready.

'No! No! Not yet!' came a desperate cry from one little group clustered close by the rail in the stern of the ship.

The Captain came striding down the deck towards them, stepping over the packed bodies.

'He said he'd be sure to come!' one man was trying to explain to the Captain. 'Give him just five more minutes, sir!'

The Captain looked with them towards the shore in the fading light.

'I can't see any sign of him,' said the Captain. He spoke quietly. 'Perhaps he's forgotten that this is the day. We can't wait much longer or we'll miss the tide.'

'He knew this was the day and he'd never forget, sir. Just five more minutes,' begged the leader of the group. They all hung over the rail, their eyes straining as they watched the blurred white road above the town.

24

'There's a horse!' cried one of the women. 'I can hear it! Listen!'

Everyone listened. The sound of hooves was beating down the track.

'It's himself!' shouted the man. 'It must be himself! How will he reach us? The gangplank's been pulled up and the rope's loose. We're drifting away already! Look at that water between us and the land!'

'Don't worry,' said the Captain. 'They'll row him out to us. He can't stay long, mind. But you'll travel better if you speak with him before we go. I know that well enough.'

Morag could see the rider now. He'd jumped down from his horse on the jetty and thrown himself into a waiting boat. He lay back recovering his strength as the men heaved on the oars and crossed the narrow strip of grey water to the ship. He was a short, bearded man in black.

The stranger seemed quite at ease on the rope ladder that was lowered down to him. He grabbed the swinging sides firmly and sprang up from rung to rung. He grasped the Captain by the hand.

'Yes, of course,' Morag heard him say. 'Five minutes. That's time enough. Thank you for waiting. I promised to come.'

The little group pressed up close to the stranger. He certainly wasn't strange to them.

'My dear people from Kilmuir,' he cried out. 'Let us hear the Word of God!' And he took a Gaelic Bible from his pocket and began at once to read to them. Now Morag knew who he must be.

The minister from Kilmuir had a strong voice. It carried right over the crowded decks as he read about the crossing of the Red Sea. It was a story they had all known for years but now it suddenly meant more to them than ever before. It had become their own story.

And the children of Israel went into the midst of the sea upon the dry ground; and the waters were a wall unto them on their right hand and on their left. Thus the Lord saved Israel that day out of the hands of the Egyptians.

When the reading was done, the minister raised his hands in prayer. Everyone on both the steamships stood up and every head was bowed as the minister gave the emigrants into God's hands.

'Be faithful, all of you!' he said when the prayer was ended. 'And in the new country, you must set up a true Free Church. Under a tree if you can't find a building! In a dry cave if you can't find a shed! And speak the Gaelic always! Teach it to your children and your grandchildren. Don't let our language die!'

The minister from Kilmuir could not hold back his own tears now.

'It's wicked!' he burst out angrily. 'They're herding you off Skye like cattle! But you'll not be forgotten! We'll be forever speaking of you here as the long years pass!'

With that he was gone. Over the side of the ship to the waiting boat. The Kilmuir families still watched him as the boat pulled away.

A shout of command rang out. Sailors sprang to the windlass. Slowly the dripping anchor rose up out of the water with a rattle of chains. A long moaning hoot came first from one ship and then from the other. Black smoke belched from the funnels. The great side-paddles churned the water. The ships shuddered.

'We're moving!' gasped Morag. 'We're leaving the Isle of Skye!'

Suddenly, without a word of direction from anyone, the familiar words of the best-loved Psalm of all rose up from one lone voice on the crowded decks. A precentor was giving out the first line of the 23rd in a powerful dirge-like chant. At once the families on both ships took up the

Psalm, singing it after the precentor, their voices swooping up high and falling down low. They swayed together as they sang and they cried as they swayed, every eye still fixed on the vanishing Island. The shepherd-people of the Isle of Skye were calling on their Shepherd-God to be with them in the valley of the shadow of death.

> *Is e Dia féin as buachaill dhomh,*
> *cha bhi mi ann an dìth*
> *Bheir e fainear gu'n luidhinn sios*
> *air cluainibh glas' le sìth.*

> *The Lord's my shepherd, I'll not want,*
> *He makes me down to lie*
> *In pastures green: He leadeth me*
> *The quiet waters by.*

The Cuillins faded from sight as the night came down. A thin sliver of a moon gleamed brilliantly among the stars. Mingled with all her sadness, Morag felt a strange new spurt of excitement. She was going to a new country on the other side of the world! High up on the poop deck, Alec Matheson was playing his fiddle. Morag smiled when she heard his tune and she sang the words softly to herself. It seemed the right kind of song for a journey.

> *May the new moon be with us wherever we go,*
> *Over the green hills and over the sea,*
> *Silver and shining, so far from our home,*
> *Over the green hills and over the sea.*

3

Old Rainy

The wind was light and the sea lay rippled and scaled under the stars. All along the decks, passive and exhausted, the people wrapped themselves up in their blankets or plaids and lay down to sleep, family by family, township by township, keeping close to the folk they knew. Occasionally a baby cried or a child coughed. Long after Alec had finished playing, Morag was still lying wide-awake as the two steamers moved steadily down between the coast and the islands, their great paddles churning a path through the sea. At last she slept.

Next morning, there was little activity along the crowded decks. The crofters from Skye seemed numbed with shock. Black bread was passed in silence from hand to hand. Janet Matheson sat smoking her pipe, pulling and puffing on the short stem and staring out blankly at the water. Alec was nursing his fiddle in his arms and rocking slowly backwards and forwards. The day grew warmer but most of the people still kept their plaids wrapped tight around their shoulders or even right over their heads. Morag was thankful that the sea was so calm. She didn't feel anything worse than a faint queasiness. The ships paused for a few hours at Oban to take on water and then steamed further south between Jura and Islay. Morag found a place with Allan by the rail where they could watch the strange green islands slipping past. Then another restless night on the open deck.

By sunrise on the second morning they'd already rounded the Mull of Kintyre and were steaming north past Arran and into the wide estuary of the River Clyde. Kirsty and Ewen sat close to Morag. She liked them both and she hardly noticed the dirty blankets they wore instead of clothes but she could never quite keep her eyes off their matted hair. It was thick with dried mud and twigs of heather and strands of grass. It was crawling with lice.

'How much longer?' wailed Kenny, pulling on his mother's hand. 'Are we nearly there?' All his earlier excitement had drained away.

'I don't know, son,' said Effie MacDonald, her voice flat and tired. 'I don't even know where we are. Donald, have you ever heard of this place we're making for? This Greenock?'

Morag's father nodded.

'I've heard of it, right enough. It's a sugar town. Full of sugar mills. And full of Highlanders too, they say. Highlanders and Irishmen. I've got a cousin living there, as a matter of fact, and I want to see him again. Iain MacDonald from Carbost. You remember him, Effie. He went off to work in Greenock years ago and his poor mother's hardly heard a word from him since. But I'm none too clear where the place is.'

Two old sailors, their faces brown and lined from years at sea, were picking their way along the deck in bare feet, stepping between the packed groups of people. A boy of about fifteen came hurrying eagerly behind them. His fair hair was bleached almost white by the sun and his eyes were a startling blue. He wore wide flapping trousers like the two older men and he had the same kind of red scarf knotted around his neck. On the outside of his right arm, stretching from elbow to wrist, was the bluish tattoo of a mermaid. Morag was just wondering whether this boy was old enough to be a sailor when suddenly he stopped.

'Greenock?' he said, grinning at the whole family, his eyes moving quickly from Donald to Allan and Morag. 'Greenock's a grand port on the River Clyde and we're nearly there!' He spoke a soft, old-fashioned Gaelic with a Lewis accent. 'You'll see a harbour full of ships from all over the world. The only thing wrong with Greenock's the rain. We call it "Old Rainy".' The boy laughed and pulled at his red scarf.

'Do you live there?' asked Morag.

'No, I live at sea most of the time now but I grew up in Greenock. I know all those little closses and alleys like the back of my hand. My father came to Greenock from Aberdeen but my mother's from the Islands. She taught me the Gaelic when I was a wee bairn.'

Donald MacDonald butted in.

'If you know the place so well, lad, perhaps you know my cousin. I must find him before we sail. His name's Iain MacDonald.'

The boy laughed again.

'There are dozens of Iain MacDonalds in Greenock! Not easy to find the right one. I suppose he works in the sugar mills.'

Donald nodded.

'I'll help you find him, if you like,' offered the boy. 'We could ask for him in the taverns. This is my last trip on the steamer so I'll have a free day when we get to Greenock.'

'Your last trip?' said Morag in surprise. 'Are you giving up the sea?'

'Not on your life! I'm changing ship at Greenock, that's all. I've been two years on these little Highland steamers, up and down the west coast. Now I want a go on the big sailing ships. I'm joining the *Georgiana* under Captain Murray. She's a beauty, that ship! Almost 700 tons! And she's sailing right to the other side of the world.'

'We know she is,' said Morag. 'We're sailing with her!'

'Are you?' The boy looked pleased. 'You're going to Victoria? I'll tell you something then.' He lowered his voice and stepped closer to Morag and Allan. He couldn't hide his excitement.

'They've found *gold* out there in that Colony! At a place called Ballarat. All the seamen in Greenock are talking about it. Everyone wants to get to the diggings. There's great gold nuggets just lying about on the ground. You only have to pick them up and then you're rich!'

'Jimmy!' bellowed one of the older seamen, coming back to look for the boy. 'Hurry up there, laddie!'

'Coming!' shouted Jimmy as he leapt along the deck. His bare feet thudded on the boards.

Allan had caught something of the boy's mood. He looked up at his father.

'Gold!' he said in amazement. 'Just lying on the ground! Could that be true?'

'Who knows?' said his father. 'But someone's sure to have picked it all up long before we get there. Don't waste your time thinking about it, Allan. That young lad's been listening to too many sailors' yarns.'

'He'll be on our ship,' said Morag, smiling 'His name's Jimmy.' Somehow the idea of sailing to the other side of the world didn't seem quite so bad.

'Greenock Ho!' came a loud voice from the bows.

Everyone rushed to starboard to catch a glimpse of the town.

When Morag first saw Greenock coming into sight across the blue water she thought it must be a town full of palaces. The morning sun was shining down onto great stone buildings, sparkling glass windows, magnificent white columns and towers and steeples. She'd never seen anything like it. It was beautiful.

'Look!' she cried. 'Mother! Look at that! Queen Victoria herself must be living there!' She edged her way through the crowd to get a better view. The pain in her ankle had eased and in all the excitement of steaming into Greenock she hardly felt it any more.

The harbours along the edge of the town were crowded with steamers and sailing ships. Masts and funnels sprouted up as thick as trees. Wharves were piled high with barrels and boxes. Teams of horses were dragging laden carts down to the docks. The sound of hammers banging on metal and wood rang out from the shipbuilding yards. Steam hissed and machines rumbled in the sugar mills. Greenock was pulsing and rocking with noise. Morag felt bewildered. She couldn't help thinking of the peace at home on Skye where the loudest sounds she ever heard were the wind and the sea.

Close up, the buildings no longer looked like palaces. Between the splendid Customs House and the fine church, Morag saw rows of squalid houses crammed close together and piled on top of each another. Washing hung from lines strung high across the narrow streets. The sky had clouded over and heavy rain began to fall. 'Old Rainy!' Morag murmured to herself. She was disappointed. Perhaps the Queen didn't live here after all.

'What do we do now?' asked a timid voice beside her. She turned and saw a tall black-haired boy. His face was white and thin and his dark eyes seemed anxious. Morag had noticed him first in the street at Portree. He was travelling with his father, a grim man who kept one hand clamped on the boy's arm most of the time as if to stop him from running away. Just now, for once, the boy was by himself. He looked as scared as Morag felt at the sight of Greenock.

'I don't know,' she answered him. 'I suppose we'll have to leave this steamer and look for the *Georgiana*. But there are so many big ships here, I don't know how we'll ever find her.'

She stared curiously at the boy.

32

'Isn't your mother travelling with you?' she asked him.

The boy seemed still more scared and he glanced over his shoulder. He shook his head but said nothing.

'Is she dead?' asked Morag bluntly.

The boy shook his head again.

'Where is she then?'

'She's out there already,' he muttered, looking down at his feet. 'In one of the Colonies. With the three little ones.'

'Come on, Morag!' Allan called impatiently from the middle of the crowd just as she was about to ask the boy more questions. 'Come and get your bundle. We're all going ashore.'

As she turned to go, the boy's father appeared suddenly at his side and grabbed his arm. His black beard bristled with anger.

'Rory!' he snarled. 'Didn't I tell you not to wander off? I've been hunting all over the ship.'

Morag was glad to get away. She wanted to know more about that boy but his father made her uneasy. Perhaps when the big ship sailed she'd find him on his own again. She eased her way through the pack to her family. All the people were flowing towards the gangway and the MacDonalds flowed with them till the solid land was under their feet again. On a wide quay in front of the high columns of the Customs House, three hundred and seventy-one men, women and children from Skye stood puzzled and uncertain, like sheep in a strange glen. Then they sat down on the ground or perched on their bundles and boxes. They kept their heads covered against the rain and waited for something to happen.

'Where's our ship?' asked Morag but no one seemed to know. Terrible rumours began to spread like wildfire through the crowd. The *Georgiana* had been lost at sea, someone said. Or she was ten days late. They'd have to camp out in the open for two weeks at least! They'd have no food to eat! Or they'd have to find lodgings in the town!

But they had so little money! They'd all catch cholera or measles or smallpox! They'd all die in Greenock! Fear and panic spread as fast as the stories.

'There's that Mr Chant!' said Morag's father in surprise. 'Look, Effie love, up on the steps!'

'Who is he?' asked Kenny, staring at the man who was climbing onto a crofter's box to address the crowd. He wore a suit of fine woollen cloth and had a new, black hat on his head. He seemed to be very pleased with himself as he gazed down at the sea of people from Skye.

'He's the emigration man, son,' said Donald. 'The one who saw us a few months back and said we could go to the Colony. And there's that other man that we saw in Portree! The man with all our names in a book!' Donald frowned at the very sight of the man who'd told them they couldn't take the dogs.

'And there's that sailor-boy, Jimmy!' cried Morag in astonishment, pointing up to the boy who stood proud and smiling on the steps beside the two men. 'What's he doing up there?'

In a minute all was clear. As Mr Chant began to speak to the crofters in his loud clear English, Jimmy translated his words sentence by sentence, into Gaelic. His voice was surprisingly strong. Everyone could hear him and they smiled at his accent. All the news was good. The *Georgiana* was ready and waiting for them just along at the West Harbour, only a few paces from where they were sitting. They could go on board straight away. There was food to eat there and a set of new clothes for every one of them. They wouldn't be sailing for three days – not till Tuesday July 13th – so they'd have time to settle in and learn the rules of the ship. They could wander around Greenock this afternoon if they liked. But Mr Chant wanted them all back on the ship by six o'clock sharp for the roll-call. That's when he'd be bringing the scissors.

'What's scissors?' asked Flora too loudly.

'I don't know,' said her mother. 'Ssshh!'

Everyone was asking the same question. 'What's scissors?'

'Probably we'll eat them!' announced Kenny confidently. 'They sound very nice.'

When Mr Chant's speech was finished, the people began to surge towards West Harbour.

'Come on!' cried Donald MacDonald. 'We don't want to be the last on board or there'll be no space left for us.'

He pushed his way through the crowd, his foot-plough grasped in his hands, and made for the tall, white ship. The families from Talisker and Carbost and Bracadale picked up their bundles and boxes for the last time and hurried after him.

The splendid new barque, *Georgiana,* towered high above them as they stood on the quay by West Harbour. Her three enormous masts stretched up towards the grey clouds and wagged in the wind. Her tapering yards were wider than the hull itself and none of her sails was spread yet. She looked like a huge bare tree in winter. Her name, *Georgiana*, stood out in letters of gold along her bow and right under the bowsprit was fixed the figurehead of a woman, carved from wood and brightly painted in red and green. She seemed to be stooping forward over the water. Morag thought the woman's bright eyes looked as if they'd be able to see the way ahead across the ocean, even in the night, and the confident smile on her smooth, white face was comforting.

'Look, Allan!' she said. 'She's smiling. Perhaps it'll be all right.'

One narrow gangway joined the ship to the quay. Donald MacDonald led his family straight up. Almost a hundred people were on before them and the line moved very slowly. At the head of the gangway sat the stern official from Portree with the Emigrant Book open in front of him. He checked every family and counted every child and looked at every paper to make sure no stowaways were creeping on board. Then he passed them on to a cheerful row of sailors who were handing out clothes. Trousers and jackets, caps and stockings, boots and plaids for the men. Thick dresses and shawls for the women and fresh white mutches to cover their heads. Warm outfits for each of the children with round snug caps for the boys and scarves and shawls for the girls. Mistress Gordon fell on her new clothes with a cry of delight. Ewen and Calum and Kirsty clutched theirs in astonishment. Morag was afraid they might start stripping off their terrible old blankets right then and there on the open deck.

'Where do we go?' asked Effie MacDonald, staring around at the seething mob in bewilderment. Allan was shouldering the box; everyone else in the family was trying to hold tight to new clothes and old bundles. Their friends from Talisker and Carbost and Bracadale kept pushing close behind.

'Straight down the companionway there!' called a bearded sailor in Gaelic, pointing to a stairway that disappeared into the bowels of the ship. 'Down in the 'tween-decks you'll find the berths, Mistress. One berth for every three or four people. Just take your pick. Single men go for'ard. Single women go aft. Behind the partitions. Families in the middle.'

'Thank you,' said Effie but she still didn't move.

'Come on, Mother!' said Morag. She stumbled towards the stairs.

At the foot of the companionway they found themselves in an enormous low room that stretched almost from one end of the ship to the other. The berths were arranged in pairs, one on top and one below, the whole way down on either side of a wide passage. In the centre of the passage was a long table with benches, all bolted to the floor. Between each pair of berths was a narrow gap, barely room enough to stand in. There were no mattresses of soft heather or grass on the berths. It was not much like home. Just bare boards and a single blanket on every bunk. The only light came from smoky lanterns that hung on cords from the ceiling.

Some families had already staked out a claim and were sitting triumphantly on their berths, unpacking their possessions and trying to settle into their own little corner of that strange vast place.

'This one'll do!' cried Allan, rushing to the nearest empty berth and flinging his box to the floor with a crash.

'No, son,' said his father. 'Let's go further along. There's much more space down there. We can find berths for Mistress Gordon and for all our Talisker families and our friends from Carbost and Bracadale too. They're only a pace or two behind us on those stairs. We must keep together.'

Allan heaved the box up to his shoulder yet again with a groan. He was tired of carrying it but he could see that his father was right.

The families moved forward towards the bow till they came to a group of empty bunks.

'Here we are!' said Donald. 'We'll take these two, one over the other. I'll go on top next to Kenny at one end and Allan can go at the other. Effie, you go here on the bottom berth. Flora can lie with Morag at the other end. Mary MacAskill, you and your family can take the two berths next to us. But Mary, make sure you go on the lower berth. You can't be climbing up and down in your condition. Mistress Gordon, you and your three children go next to the MacAskills. Two at the foot and two at the head. Neil MacKinnon, your family can go on top of the Gordons. The Mathesons can take the next two berths and the MacInnes family in the two after that. Now you good folk from Carbost'll come next and all the Bracadale families can go along the other side, just across the way from us.

That's fine! Now we're all together. And if God wills it, we'll stay safely together till the journey's end.'

Allan thumped down his box at last. Morag lay flat on the lower berth. Her mother sat beside her and began to cry.

'Donald!' she said through her tears. 'We're really leaving. We can't turn back now. And these berths are so open. Everyone'll stare at us when we go to bed at night.'

'Let's unpack, Effie love,' he said gently, an arm around her shoulder at once. 'It's so dark in here with those smoky lanterns that I don't think anyone'll be able to see anyone else. But we could hang a blanket from the edge of the top berth here. Then you'll feel more private underneath. It'll be as safe as our little black house on Skye.'

The very mention of the little black house made Effie cry harder than ever but she opened the box and untied the bundles and spread their goods and chattels on the bunk to look at them again. She held the Bible in her arms for a minute and then found a place for it to rest by the head of the bunk up above.

'If I put a folded skirt on top of the Bible, it'll make a fine pillow for you, Donald,' she said, pleased with the idea.

Donald was hanging his pouch of black earth on a hook. He turned round and shook his head.

'We can't treat the Good Book like a pillow, Effie! Let's wrap it in your best skirt and slide it into that little space underneath the bottom berth. We can put our box and this foot-plough in the hold tomorrow. All our things'll be safe for the whole voyage. No one from Skye would steal from another.'

'Don't be so sure of that, Donald MacDonald!' said a man's harsh voice from just beyond the Bracadale families. 'I've known wicked thieves right on the Isle of Skye! And I've made sure they were punished too!'

38

It was the tall, dark boy's father. The boy himself stood trembling beside the bottom bunk where they had just put their few possessions. Morag tried to catch his eye but he didn't look up. His gaze was fixed on the floorboards.

'Angus MacRae!' exclaimed Donald MacDonald in delight, grasping the man's hand. 'Angus MacRae from Kilbeg! I haven't seen you these ten years or more! And is this your son?'

Angus MacRae nodded but with no sign of pleasure.

'Rory's his name,' he said.

One of the sailors came pushing his way down past the long table, checking that every berth was full and that no one had taken too much space.

'Sorry,' he said, stopping by the MacRae's berth. 'You can't stay here. This part of the ship's just for families.'

'We *are* a family!' said Angus MacRae bitterly. 'This boy is my son!'

'How old's the boy?' asked the sailor, peering at him.

'Only just fifteen.'

'Sorry. There's no wife with you. You don't count as a family. You'll both have to go with the single men. Right up near the fo'csle. It's through that partition just ahead of you. All boys over fourteen have to go in there with the single men.'

Angus MacRae muttered to himself. He and Rory took up their bundles again and walked slowly forward to the single men's section, through a studded door in the thick partition. The sailor's eyes swept over the crowd searching for any other boys over fourteen. The MacDonalds froze and held their breath. Allan had turned fourteen but he did look younger. Ewen Gordon might be fourteen too. It was hard to tell how old those puny Gordon children really were. The sailor didn't seem to notice Allan or Ewen. Morag breathed again. She knew Allan wouldn't want to go through that door with a lot of strangers. She felt sorry for Rory, imprisoned in there with his father.

Calum Gordon had his new clothes on! The blanket had gone! He went skipping down between the berths to show everyone, turning this way and that, pausing every few minutes to stroke the cloth of his warm jacket.

'Look!' he shouted to Morag. 'And look at these things here!' He fished something out of his pocket and held them in front of her eyes.

'What are they?' asked Morag.

'The sailor told me they're a knife and a fork. We're supposed to eat our food with them.'

Everyone laughed and rushed up to see the knife and fork.

'Look in your own pockets,' said Calum. 'The pockets of your new clothes. There's a knife and a fork for everyone and soon we'll be given a tin plate and a pannikin too.'

'But we don't need a thing like that for eating!' exclaimed Allan in astonishment, taking Calum's fork in his hand and turning it this way and that. 'What's wrong with our fingers?'

'I don't know,' laughed Calum. 'I'm only telling you what the sailor said.'

Now Jimmy came pushing through the crowded 'tween-decks.

'Donald MacDonald!' he called out. 'Do you want to come and look for that cousin of yours in the town? I'm going ashore. You can all come with me if you like.'

Effie shook her head.

'I don't want to wander around Greenock,' she said firmly. 'It looks a dangerous place to me. I'm staying here and Flora and Kenny'll stay with me.'

'I'll come!' said Allan.

'Me too!' said Morag.

'You'd better tie a bit of cloth around your mouth,' said Jimmy seriously. 'I never bother with it myself because I'm used to the place. But there's a lot of sickness in Greenock and some folk say it's safer to cover up your mouth.'

'I thought sickness came from touching,' said Morag in surprise, hunting for her white scarf and giving Allan a square of blue cloth for a gag.

'That's just what my mother says,' answered Jimmy. 'But my father says it comes from eating bad food. No one really knows. It's better to be safe than sorry. Now come on and we'll hunt for that Iain McDonald of yours.'

Allan and Morag went off at once with their father and Jimmy. The rain had stopped and the day was warm and sultry. Donald refused to walk through the town with a ridiculous rag tied over his mouth but Morag and Allan were quite proud of theirs.

'Jimmy,' she mumbled at him through the cloth as they hurried over the quay. 'Why were you doing that translating for Mr Chant up on the steps? Does he know you?'

'I can't understand a word you're saying,' laughed Jimmy.

She pulled off the scarf and asked him again.

'No, I've never seen him in my life before,' said Jimmy. 'But he called out for someone who knew the Gaelic as well as the English so I just ran up and said I could do it for him.'

'You did it well, lad,' said Donald.

Morag smiled at Jimmy before she covered her mouth again.

'Yes,' she said. 'You did.'

Katie

The stench in Greenock was terrible. The narrow streets
were choked with mud and filth. Foul, stinking rubbish,
thrown out from the houses overnight, still lay in heaps up
every alley. Soon Morag's bare feet were black with slime.
Long lines of haggard women, shawls over their heads,
waited outside the pawnbroker's shops, each one of them
clutching a pair of shoes, a blunt knife or a chipped brown
teapot to exchange over the counter for a few pennies.

'They get their things back on pay-day,' explained
Jimmy. 'They need the money now for food. Or for the
drink. Everyone lives like that here. It's the only way.'

They passed a lodging house called 'The Shamrock'.
Loud singing and shouting burst out through the open
door. Drunken men and women reeled away from noisy
taverns, clinging to the walls or simply falling straight down
into the mud. No one stopped to pick them up. Gangs of
grimy children pushed and shoved. Morag felt a deft hand
sliding into her pocket. She grabbed at her small white shell
to keep it safe and she struck out wildly at the thief. A child
screamed and spat and ran off down an alley.

'We'll ask in here,' said Jimmy, quite untroubled by the
smell and the noise. He turned aside to a crowded inn and
elbowed his way through the bellowing mass of drinkers
to speak to the landlord. In a few minutes he was out again,
gasping for breath.

'He says we should try the 'Prince Charlie'. Just on the next corner. That's where the Skyemen drink.'

The 'Prince Charlie' was even worse than the first place. Jimmy pushed in through the crowd again. Morag heard an old Gaelic song that she knew so well from home, roared out through drunken throats. It sounded different here.

'The landlord knows two of them,' said Jimmy emerging again, red in the face from all his heaving and shoving. 'One stays in a lodging house up the next closs. The other's in Ann Street in a room over the bootmaker's shop.'

Suddenly, without warning, a terrible roaring and whistling filled the air. The buildings around them seemed to shake. Morag clutched at Jimmy's arm.

'What is it?' she gasped, her voice muffled by the cloth around her mouth.

'That's just the blower for twelve o'clock,' said Jimmy. 'All the mills let off their hooters at noon. Now the men who're lucky enough to have work go home to eat some bread and swallow some whisky before they start on the afternoon shift.'

In an instant the streets were packed tighter still by the men rushing home from the mills and the docks, their pinched white faces streaked with grease. Jimmy shepherded the MacDonalds out of the way and into a narrow passage off the street. Allan stumbled straight into a pile of fish bones and mushy wet grey rubbish.

'Ugh!' he shouted and sprang back in horror.

'I hate this place!' Morag whispered to him.

'This way!' said Jimmy cheerfully and he led them to a rickety outer stair and up to a door on the first floor. Inside a dark passage there were more doors and more stairs. Up and up they climbed in single file, each of them holding on tight to the one in front. At the top of the last stair there were two doors. Jimmy knocked on one of them.

'Iain MacDonald!' he called. 'Are you there? Open up, man! Cousins from Skye here to see you.'

The door opened just a crack and an old man's face peered out at them.

'Who wants Iain MacDonald?' he croaked.

'I do,' said Donald. 'I'm looking for my cousin. Iain MacDonald from Carbost on Skye. Do you know him at all?'

'I *am* Iain MacDonald!' said the man. 'But I don't come from Skye. Now get out of here quick. We've got the sickness.' And he slammed the door.

They turned and fled down the stairs and out into the street again.

'We'll try the bootmaker next,' said Jimmy. 'Laurence Kay in Ann Street.'

'I want to go back to the ship,' stammered Morag. 'I feel sick. I think I'm getting cholera!'

'Don't be silly, girl,' said her father.

Ann Street was narrow. Shops and houses were crammed close together. The bootmaker's door stood open and Mr Kay himself, a wiry little man in a leather apron, was hammering away vigorously at his last on the sole of a large black boot. A pair of steel-rimmed spectacles sat on the end of his nose and jumped with each blow of the hammer. A plump girl of about fourteen was sorting through a stack of broken boots and shoes, finding the next pair for him to tackle when the black boots were done.

'Can I help you?' asked the bootmaker courteously, pausing in his work. The little shop was quiet after the violent hurly-burly of the streets. Morag hoped he wouldn't notice her slimy feet. But he did notice the rag tied around her face.

'You'll be from one of the ships,' he said with a smile. 'Ship people are always nervous about sickness in Greenock.'

Morag caught sight of a row of books on a shelf behind

44

the bootmaker's bench. One of them looked very much like a Bible to her though she couldn't read the strange English words along the spine. The cover was good black leather. She nudged her father and pointed. He looked at the book too and nodded with satisfaction.

Jimmy spoke up in English.

'We're looking for an Iain MacDonald from Skye,' he said.

Mr Laurence Kay put down his hammer. His face was suddenly serious.

'We do have an Iain MacDonald staying in the back room upstairs,' he said. 'And yes, he does come from Skye. A placed called Carbost.'

'That's my cousin!' exclaimed Donald MacDonald excitedly as he heard the word 'Carbost'. 'Where is he?'

'He's sick,' said the bootmaker, and Jimmy translated his words as he spoke. 'Not the cholera or anything like that. It's his lungs. Galloping consumption! His poor wife died from the same thing nine months back and left him with a new-born child. A whining, wizened little creature it is too. Not long for this world, I'd say. Do you want to see him?'

Donald MacDonald nodded but he didn't look quite so keen now.

'I'll step up and ask him,' said Mr Kay and he went out through a door at the back of the shop. The bootmaker's daughter was staring at Morag and Allan.

'Are you off to the Colonies?' she asked them eagerly.

Jimmy translated again. He was quick. He slipped from one language to the other like a fish darting from river to sea and back again when the tide is at the full.

'We are,' said Allan. 'To a Colony in Australia. They used to call it Port Phillip but it's Victoria now.'

'Because of the Queen,' explained Morag, pulling down her scarf to speak more clearly.

45

'That's exactly where *I* want to go!' cried the girl. 'Victoria! It sounds like heaven to me!'

'You *want* to go there!' exclaimed Allan in amazement as soon as he'd understood what she was saying.

'Yes, don't *you* want to go? There's gold out there! You're lucky to be off so soon. We've got to wait another six months till we can get a berth on a ship. And we have to pay our own way. You crofters from the Islands get a passage to the Colony for nothing at all!'

'Is your father going too?' asked Morag, suddenly interested. 'Does he know that all the feet are turned round the wrong way out there? He'll have trouble making back-to-front boots, won't he?'

The girl laughed as Jimmy put the words into English.

'We've heard that story too,' she said, 'but it's not true. We're going to find a wonderful new life for ourselves. We're going to find gold! Aren't you looking forward to it all?'

When they had grasped her question, Morag and Allan shook their heads. They could hardly believe that anyone would actually *want* to sail away to Victoria, let alone pay out good money for the fare. But Morag couldn't help catching something of the girl's excitement.

The bootmaker came into the shop again and beckoned them forward.

Jimmy led the MacDonalds out through the back door and they followed Mr Kay along a passageway, up some squeaky wooden stairs to a small bare landing. At least this house was clean. There was no smell here except the pleasant reek of leather from the shop below. The bootmaker pointed to a closed door.

'He's in there,' he said and he left them.

Donald knocked on the door.

'Iain? It's your cousin Donald from Talisker here!'

'Come in!' called a faint voice.

Jimmy opened the door. Iain MacDonald lay on a bed of straw. A grey blanket covered his body. He was a young man, bony and gaunt, with flaming hectic cheeks and sick bright eyes. He was seized by a fit of coughing the minute he saw them but as the cough subsided he held out his shaking hands to Donald.

'Cousin!' he sobbed and tears began to pour down his face. 'You've come at last!'

Donald rushed forward and flung his arms around him.

'Iain! You're sick, man! Terribly sick! Why ever didn't you write home to Carbost? Why didn't you take the steamship back to Skye again? Your poor mother hasn't heard a word from you for years. She grieves for you, Iain! You shouldn't be lying here in a strange town with no one to look after you at all!'

'It's not a strange town to me,' gasped Iain between new bouts of coughing. He shivered. 'Though I hate the place. I've been here a long time. Ten years. Twelve years. I forget how long. Ever since I was fifteen. Don't ask me why I didn't go home. I don't know why. The bootmaker's family here takes good care of me. But I can't last much longer. You've arrived just in time, Donald. I've prayed every day for someone to come from home. Who told you? How did you know that I needed you?'

'I didn't know,' said Donald. 'We're sailing for the Colony in a few days. We've been cleared off the croft. I came to say goodbye.'

'Goodbye it is,' said Iain, still clinging desperately to Donald's two hands.

The thin cry of a child came from a corner of the tiny room.

Morag spun round. A baby, well-wrapped up against the cold, lay on a straw-stuffed pillow. She picked up the child.

'Morag! Take care!' said Donald MacDonald. 'The baby might be sick too!'

The baby certainly looked sick. Its sunken eyes were closed. The skin of its face was tight.

'What's its name?' asked Morag, coming up to Iain's bed.

'Catriona,' he said. 'I call her Katie. That was what Silis wanted. Silis was my wife. She's dead.'

Morag stroked the baby's cheek.

'Katie!' she said quietly.

The eyelids flickered open. The eyes gazed up uncertainly at Morag's face. Katie began to cry again, a weak strangled cry.

'She needs some milk,' said Morag.

Iain pointed to a cup on the window-ledge. Morag began to spoon the cold milk into the baby's open mouth. Katie dribbled and spat as much as she swallowed but at least the sad crying had stopped.

'I found her a wet-nurse for the first seven months,' said Iain. 'But now the wet-nurse is sick herself. She had to send Katie back to me a few weeks ago. So I just try to feed her with the spoon. You can see she doesn't swallow much. That's why she's thin.'

Morag kept feeding the baby till the cup was empty.

'Donald!' said Iain, his voice cracked and desperate. He struggled to sit up. 'Will you take the child?'

'Take the child? To the Colony? No! It's impossible!'

'What will become of her?' cried Iain. 'In a few days from now I'll be dead. The doctor says it's a week at the most. Silis has gone. What will become of the child?'

'Father! Why can't we take her?' said Morag, hugging Katie tighter in her arms.

'I'll tell you why, Morag,' said her father gently. 'We'd have to pay a fare for her and we've only got a few shillings. You know that. And she could be sick. Just look at her face! The doctor on the ship would never let us bring her on board. Her sickness could spread. People might die from whatever it is. *You* might die, Morag. Now do you understand?'

'But Father, we needn't tell anyone!' said Allan, taking up Morag's plea with sudden urgency. 'No one will notice one extra baby among all those children on the ship! We could just pretend she's our little sister. And we needn't say she's sick! That'd be stupid. Mother'll soon nurse her back to health again.'

Donald MacDonald groaned. His voice was suddenly stern.

'Allan! I've been trying to bring you up to be truthful and honest. And now you're saying we should tell a pack of lies. We can't possibly pretend that this baby is our baby. We can't possibly smuggle her on board and pretend she isn't sick. That's not right and you know it!'

'But it's not right to leave her here to die, is it?' cried Morag, shocked and angry. 'Far from Skye and in a house of strangers! That's much worse than telling a lie.'

'They're good people in this house,' said her father. 'Godly people. I saw the Bible downstairs. Let her be their child!'

'But she's a MacDonald!' said Iain from his bed. 'She's part of your family. She's your own flesh and blood. Just look at her hair, Donald! It's the colour of yours.'

Morag looked. The baby had hardly any hair at all but what little there was of it was certainly red. And her blue eyes were strangely like Flora's.

Jimmy spoke now.

'Why don't we take the child to the Captain on the *Georgiana* and see what he says. I can talk to him for you. I'm one of his crew now, even though I'm the youngest of them all. Everyone says Captain Murray's a good man. He might let you pay the fare back later. He could ask the Surgeon to look at her first. Just to make sure all's well.'

Donald MacDonald hesitated. Morag held her breath and looked down at Katie.

'Please, Donald!' begged Iain, lying back on the straw, weak with exhaustion. 'Your father and my father were brothers! Katie belongs to you already. Look how well your daughter holds her! Take her! Give her a chance to live!'

Donald MacDonald put his head in his hands.

'All right,' he said at last. 'We'll see what the Captain says. But if he won't take the child, I'll be back with her tonight, Iain.'

Iain nodded. He couldn't speak. Morag put down the baby for a minute. One by one, she and Allan and their father came up close to the bed and hugged Iain to say goodbye. Then Morag took up the baby again and they all hurried from the room with Jimmy close behind them.

'So you'll take the child?' asked the bootmaker when he saw them, relief plain in his voice and his face.

'If the Captain agrees, I'll take her,' said Donald. 'If not, I'll be back with her tonight. Mr Kay, I want to thank you for all you've done for my cousin.'

'I'll see he's well buried,' said the bootmaker. 'He won't go into a pauper's grave. You can rest easy about that.'

'Goodbye!' said his daughter to Morag. 'I might see you in the Colony one day. On the gold-diggings! Who knows?'

They left the shop, Morag still carrying the baby.

Back on the ship, Donald sent Allan down below to tell his mother what had happened. Jimmy brought a bucket of cold water so that he and Morag and Donald could wash the slime of Greenock off their feet before they faced the Captain.

'He likes a clean ship,' said Jimmy. 'That's what I've heard. Now we'll find the Chief Mate, Mr Boyd. If we can talk him round, then perhaps he'll take us up to Captain Murray himself.'

Mr Boyd heard the story and looked at the sickly child, quiet and still now in Morag's arms. He shook his head doubtfully.

'It's a sad tale, right enough. I'd like to help you but I'm not sure that Captain Murray'll agree to it. He won't mind about the fare. It's the sickness he'll be worried about. An ailing baby from Greenock is the last kind of passenger he'll be wanting on board. If that poor child is sickening for typhus or cholera or even measles or whooping cough, just think how it could run through the ship. We'd be heaving dead bodies overboard every night after dark.'

Morag shuddered when she'd heard Jimmy's translation.

'But if the Surgeon saw the baby first, sir,' persisted Jimmy. 'Maybe he could tell if anything's seriously wrong.'

Mr Boyd agreed. He took them to the cabin of the Surgeon-Superintendent. Mr Gilby didn't look pleased to be interrupted. He was sitting in a comfortable chair and puffing on a long-stemmed pipe. But he set his pipe to one side, laid the baby on his table and bent down over her. He stripped off all her clothes and examined every limb, peered into her mouth and ears, listened to her chest, tapped her and turned her. The bones of her rib-cage stood out in the tiny body. She reminded Morag of a small sea-bird, blown ashore on Skye by the winter wind.

'She's not actually sickening for anything as far as I can see, Mr Boyd,' he said at last, straightening his back and handing the naked baby back to Morag to dress again. 'There's no fever. It's starvation she's suffering from. She needs careful feeding. Milk and porridge six times a day. If someone's prepared to spoon the stuff into her and keep her warm, she might recover.'

'I'll do it,' said Morag quickly, as Jimmy translated. 'And our mother knows all about babies.'

'Well, I'll write you a note for the Captain.' He scribbled on a sheet of white paper. 'You take this family up there, Mr Boyd. Jimmy, you can go too – just for translating in case Donald MacDonald can't make himself understood. The Captain's a Highlander and he's proud of it but he doesn't know the Gaelic. Mind you keep a civil tongue in your head, boy, and don't speak unless Captain Murray speaks to you first. You're the most junior member of this ship's crew, remember.'

'Aye aye, sir,' said Jimmy politely. 'I know my place, sir.'

Mr Boyd led them aft along the spar deck and up the last set of steps. He tapped gently on the door of the Captain's cabin. Morag felt nervous now. She wondered if she should curtsey.

'Take your cap off, Father,' she whispered.

Donald MacDonald looked startled but he whipped off his black cap just in time as the door opened. Captain Murray was a big man. He towered over the Mate and Jimmy. To Morag's relief, he smiled as he saw the group outside his door.

'What's all this, Mr Boyd?' he said. 'A deputation? No complaints already, surely. We haven't even set sail yet.'

'No sir,' said the Mate. 'It's not a complaint. Just a request, sir. About this baby.' He pushed Morag forward, handed over the Surgeon's note and told the whole story once again. Captain Murray looked at the baby and then he looked at Jimmy.

'Aren't you the new ship's-boy? What do you have to do with all this?'

'I took this family to see their cousin, sir,' he said, his voice soft and respectful. 'We had to hunt for him in Greenock you see, sir, and I could translate for them. I speak the Gaelic, you see, sir. From my mother.'

'You speak the Gaelic? Well, that could be useful. Here we've got a whole shipload of Skye emigrants with hardly a word of decent English between the lot of them! I might well need you on the voyage, boy. Who else speaks the Gaelic, Mr Boyd? Among the crew, I mean.'

'MacDougall, sir, and MacNeill. That's all, sir.'

'Mmm. MacDougall and MacNeill. What's your name again, laddie?'

'Jimmy, sir. Jimmy MacLean.'

'Right, Jimmy MacLean. Be ready to come when I need you.'

'Aye aye, sir!' said Jimmy, grinning with pride.

'But what will we be doing about this baby, Captain Murray?' said Donald MacDonald in his stiff English with the distinctive Highland lilt to it. He wanted the Captain to know that at least one Skye crofter on board could manage a bit of the strange southern tongue.

'Ah yes, the baby. I'd forgotten. All right. You can bring her on board. And you needn't pay a fare. She won't cost us much, will she? A handful of oatmeal and a few cups of milk a day. We've got three good cows out there on the deck, in a neat little pen under a couple of lifeboats. The carpenter's rigged it up for me. I've had the Surgeon's word that nothing's wrong with the child that good food won't put right.'

'Yes, sir. Thank you, sir,' said the Chief Mate and turned to go. Morag stood waiting a minute by the door as her father and Mr Boyd walked away down the deck. She could hear their footsteps growing fainter.

'What is it, lassie?' said the Captain, smiling down on her. 'Speak up now. Jimmy here will tell me what you're wanting to say.'

'Sir,' said Morag hesitantly. 'I was just wondering if you could give me a pen and a wee bottle of ink, please. It's for writing home to the minister in Carbost. He said to be sure to ask you.'

Jimmy nearly exploded. His face was red with embarrassment. He turned on Morag.

'You can't ask him that!' he said. 'He's the Captain!'

'What's she saying, Jimmy MacLean?' asked Captain Murray.

Reluctantly Jimmy told him.

The Captain tipped back his head and roared with laughter.

'A pen and a wee bottle of ink!' he exclaimed. 'Well,

why not? The minister's quite right. You *should* write home to him, lassie.'

He stepped back into his cabin and reached up to a cupboard over his head. It was well-stocked with bottles of ink. He took out the smallest and gave it to Morag. He gave her a newly-cut pen from his desk.

'Thank you, sir,' she said, holding the baby and the ink and the pen very tight. 'May the good Lord bless you, sir, and give us a safe voyage.'

Jimmy translated, still flushed and troubled by all this conversation.

'Amen to that,' said the Captain, smiling at her still. 'Now take that poor bairn down to your mother, lassie.'

Effie MacDonald took Katie from Morag's arms and looked at her carefully.

'We'll feed her well, Morag. If God wills it, she'll recover. She'd better sleep next to you in the bottom berth. Flora can move to my end. Mind you don't overlay that baby, now. She's such a tiny wee thing. But she's got the look of a true MacDonald about her face.'

'Roll-call!' shouted a grey-bearded sailor from the companionway. Perhaps that's the one called MacDougall, thought Morag. Or perhaps it's MacNeill. His Gaelic was good. 'Everyone up to the quarter-deck! Children too! Hurry! The Captain's waiting!'

'What's the quarter-deck?' everyone was asking everyone else.

'I know,' said Allan. 'Jimmy told me. It's behind the main mast. Come on!' And he led the hordes of emigrants up one stairway after another to the quarter-deck where the Captain stood in a wide space between the lifeboats, the thick Emigrant Book in his hands. Mr Chant was beside him with two strong wooden boxes. Next to Mr Chant stood a small man in a huge white apron. Next to him again was a stout woman in a neat cap and a plain brown

54

dress. Jimmy MacLean stood close at hand, ready to translate.

The roll-call took a long, long time. There were so many Donald MacDonalds on board. So many Alec Mathesons. So many Neil MacKinnons. So many Ewen Gordons. So many Camerons and Campbells, MacPhersons and MacPhees, Nicolsons and Bethunes, McKays and Grants. Every family had to be identified by the township they came from as well as by name. At last it was done. The Captain had even added Katie MacDonald's name to the family from Talisker. Three hundred and seventy-two emigrants and a crew of twenty-three.

'And now, Mr Chant has something to say to you all,' said the Captain and he stepped to one side.

Mr Chant looked immensely proud as he surveyed this vast crowd of emigrants that his own Society was sending off to the Colony. First he introduced the woman. She was the Matron.

'She'll look after you well,' said Mr Chant, through Jimmy's translation. 'Especially the women and children and anyone who's sick. She speaks no Gaelic, of course, but that won't matter a scrap.'

Laughter broke out at this from the crowded deck. How was she going to take care of them if she couldn't understand what they wanted to say to her? The Matron was clearly annoyed at the sudden burst of laughter. She frowned. She put her plump white hands on her hips and stared back at the people.

'And now for the scissors!' cried Mr Chant, stooping to open one of his boxes. A buzz of excitement went through the crowd. 'A pair of scissors for every family and one between six for the single folk.'

He held up a large pair of black scissors. Everyone gazed at them.

'And the wonderful thing is that you can keep them when the voyage is done! Along with some Gaelic Psalm books I've brought along for everyone. Presents from the Emigration Society for this splendid ship-load of people from Skye.'

The crowd muttered around him. Jimmy explained.

'They don't know what the scissors are for, sir,' he said politely.

'I'm just going to show you,' said Mr Chant. 'I didn't think you knew much about scissors or you never would have come on board looking like a herd of wild Highland cattle, would you?' And he laughed at his own little joke.

'Come here, boy!' he said, beckoning to Ewen Gordon who happened to be in the front row. 'You're one of the worst. Just sit on this box where everyone can see you.'

Ewen seemed quite pleased to be picked out for something special. He liked showing off his new clothes. He climbed up on the box and grinned down at everyone.

Mr Chant waved forward the short man in the white apron and handed him the scissors.

'Go ahead, Balfour,' he said.

Tam Balfour, the barber from Glasgow, grasped the scissors firmly in his right hand. He put his other hand on Ewen's shoulder. He cocked his head first on one side and then on the other, surveying the tangled mop of filthy hair with a look of distaste. Then with a few sudden deft clips he cut Ewen's hair all the way round. A gasp of astonishment rose up from the emigrants as the dirty black hair fell to the deck. Ewen himself let out a cry of rage.

'Sit still, boy,' said Mr Chant sharply. 'The barber hasn't finished with you yet.'

The barber kept snipping away at Ewen's hair till the boy was almost unrecognizable.

'That'll give you all the general idea,' said Mr Chant. 'Now we'll see if we can do something about those terrible beards. You can get down, boy.' Ewen was only too glad to escape, his hands clamped tight on his short hair. 'You'll do,' and Mr Chant grabbed at an old man whose magnificent white beard hung down to his waist.

The old man protested but he had to sit on the box. The barber wielded his scissors again. In a few minutes the beard was neat and short. The old man climbed sadly down again and went back to his family. He didn't look himself at all. His grandchildren stared up at him with puzzled eyes.

Morag heard her father quoting a line from the Bible behind her.

' "As the sheep before her shearers is dumb",' he murmured bitterly. ' "So he opened not his mouth." That's what we are. Nothing but sheep in the hands of the shearers!'

'Now,' said Mr Chant triumphantly, 'every family can come out here and get a pair of scissors. The barber will help anyone who can't manage for himself. Oh, I almost forgot! There's something more for you in the other box.'

He bent to lift something up out of the second box.

'Brushes!' he cried, brandishing a large hair-brush above his head. 'One for every family and one between six for the single folk. Another generous gift from your Emigration Society.'

One by one, the fathers of each family came slowly forward to claim their scissors, their Gaelic Psalm book and their hair-brush.

'No supper till the hair's cut short!' shouted Mr Chant.

The sound of clicking scissors filled the air. The barber moved from family to family, lending a skilled hand wherever it was needed, but most people preferred to do the work themselves. Soon the open deck was littered with hair – black and brown, fair and red, with a few heaps of grey hair and white. Every beard was cut short and square. The people gazed at each other in amazement. No one seemed to be quite the same. Morag pushed her fingers through what was left of her own dark hair. She felt sad. It seemed to her to be a strange way to be starting the voyage to an unknown country on the other side of the world.

5

Sailing South

Three days later, the *Georgiana* sailed. The ship had begun
to feel less strange and bewildering now to Morag and
Allan. There were more than a hundred and thirty children
on board with them, running up and down the com-
panionways, climbing over the bunks, finding corners on
the open decks where they could play, making new friends
from all over Skye.

Dr Norman MacLeod, the 'Friend of Highlanders,' came
from Glasgow to preach them out on the 13th July, bringing copies of the Shorter Catechism in Gaelic and English.
He told them they were setting off, like Abraham of old,
for a new and better country. When the people had sung
their hearts out yet again with the 23rd Psalm, and the
minister had gone ashore, two noisy steamtugs eased the
ship away from the dock and out into the wide stream of
the Clyde. Slowly she edged her way down river, all her
sails still furled and her spars bare. The emigrants stood
thick along the deck and gazed hungrily at the land.

The tugs had pulled the *Georgiana* well down beyond
the last tip of Bute before they let her go. Hooting cheerfully, they turned and chugged back to Greenock as the
Captain and the Mate shouted their orders to the crew.
The sailors' bare feet pounded along the deck. Morag
craned her head to look aloft at the tangle of ropes and
shrouds and yards and at the tiny figures of seamen clam-

bering about as agile as the fulmars balancing on their nests on the cliffs of Skye. Her heart was in her mouth in case a foot should slip and a sailor pitch to his death on the deck but no one fell. Jimmy himself was up there. Her eye was on him. He waved down to her.

A fine wind sprang up behind. With a bellowed order from the Mate and a great cry from aloft and below, the sails were loosed, the yards were braced, and the ship began to move steadily down past Arran. The new white canvas cracked and billowed in the wind and the ropes rattled against the masts. Gently at first but then more strongly, the ship began to roll. The voyage to the Colony had begun.

Neil MacKinnon found a place for himself and his pipes high on the quarter-deck. Morag could see him clearly. Then she heard the familiar sound of the drones as he filled his bag with air, tucked it under his arm and played a few notes on his chanter to settle the pipes down comfortably. All the people were suddenly quiet, turning to watch him and waiting for the tune they knew would come. Neil launched into the pibroch, a lament for leaving home. 'Cha Till Mi Tuilleadh – I shall return no more!' They knew it was true. They would never see Scotland again.

When the pibroch had ended, Morag suddenly became aware that the deck was tipping beneath her. Her stomach lurched. She clung tight to the rail in front of her and gasped in huge lungfuls of salty air. Just behind her, in the lee of a lifeboat, two seamen were talking quietly together in Gaelic. They must be MacDougall and MacNeill, she thought to herself. She listened.

'Have you ever seen a worse rabble than this lot?' one man muttered with a gruff laugh. 'They don't seem quite so bad now but did you get a good look at the terrible rags they were wearing when they came aboard? And the stink of them! They looked like a pack of wild animals till that barber got to work with his scissors!'

'And some of them seem to be half-starved,' said the other, his lighter voice more troubled than scornful. 'I was watching them wolf down their porridge this morning. That gave me a shock, John. It's so long since I left the Highlands. I didn't know things were as bad as all that.'

'Didn't you ever hear about it? It's been worst of all on the Islands. They've had the blight up there. They've had the famine. They've had the cholera. And now they're being cleared off the land. Lucky we got out when we did, Walter. A life at sea's hard enough but at least we get food in our stomachs.'

'What do you make of that Jimmy MacLean?'

'What? The new boy? He seems all right. He's been at sea for a couple of years. He has the Gaelic, you know. Like us.'

'That's just the trouble, John. He's far too friendly with Mr Boyd and the Captain for my liking. They're always calling on him for the translating but by rights it should be one of us! The boy's only fifteen! We're twice his age and our English is just as good.'

'Do you reckon he'll be joining us when we all run off to the gold-diggings?' whispered the deeper voice. 'Our plan'll never go well if that boy's against us. He'll hear us talking with the other men in the fo'c'sle and before we know what's up he'll have told the Captain everything. Then we'll never get away to Ballarat and the gold.'

'There's only one thing to do. Make sure he hears none of our talk. Till we're more certain of him, anyway. I'll speak to the Bosun and Jamie Cross, the cook. Jamie Cross is the key man. He'll soon tell the rest of the men to keep their mouths shut tight when that Jimmy's around.'

'When we're well south of Ireland, I'll try to have a talk with the boy. Quiet-like. Sound him out. See if he wants to go for the gold. He's a good lad, really. I'd like him to join us.'

'Don't give away too much, John!'

'I won't. Don't worry! Not till we're sure of him.'

'John MacNeill!' roared the Captain from the door of his cabin. 'Where are you?'

'Here, sir!' called the deep voice, switching from Gaelic to English.

'Find me the Steward and ask him to step this way. And be quick about it!'

'Aye aye, sir.'

Morag turned her head now to look. One of the men was running off to search for the Steward. He was short. He had black hair and a black beard. So that must be John MacNeill. The gruff one. And the other sailor, thin and stooping, with the scraggy red beard and the softer voice – that must be Walter MacDougall. She wondered if Jimmy would want to run off to the diggings with these sailors. Would Allan be joining them too? As the ship shuddered under her feet, she felt her way carefully down the stairs.

The ship's violent motion soon made heads spin and stomachs churn. The people stretched their hands out blindly to their bunks and lay down, letting the nausea sweep over them in terrible waves. Only a few lucky ones seemed quite unaffected. Mistress Gordon was walking around proudly in her new clothes as if nothing were the matter. Flora and Kenny were laughing together at some game of their own as they crawled underneath the long table. Alec Matheson seemed perfectly well. He had unwrapped his fiddle and he sat on his berth and began to play a cheerful jig.

'Oh stop, stop!' moaned Janet beside him. 'I can't bear that noise. Put it away, Alec. Go up on the deck if you feel so full of life. This is a hospital down here. It's no place for jigging!'

Things grew far worse as night came down. The wind blew stronger and a thunderstorm broke overhead. The ship began to pitch and toss as it rolled, heaving its prow high out of the water and then plunging heavily down

61

again. Fear as well as sea-sickness was gripping the emigrants now as they lay there shivering and groaning, tightly packed in the narrow berths, one sweating body pressed against another. Tin plates and pannikins fell off the table and rattled from one side of the ship to the other. No one had the strength to climb off the bunks and gather them up again.

Morag lifted her head and looked down the long, dark rows. The smoking lamps swung from side to side on their cords, giving out a feeble yellow light and an unpleasant stink of oil. The timbers of the vessel creaked and shuddered. The sea knocked loudly outside and seemed to Morag to be frighteningly close. Now more than three hundred people were not just feeling ill; they were being sick. Some managed to find a pot to be sick into; others were sick on the floor, on the blankets, in the bunk, all over their clothes. Babies cried. Children screamed between bouts of violent retching. Some of the mothers tried, in the semi-darkness, to wipe up the mess, to hold the heads of those who were vomiting, but there was little they could do. In the end they simply climbed back into their bunks and lay down again. The fearful smell of ship's bilge and other people's sickness filled Morag's nostrils. Appalling noises filled her ears.

'Allan,' she whispered, turning the shivering Katie onto one side and wiping her own face on the grey blanket.

'What is it?' groaned Allan from the top bunk.

'Did you know it would be like this?'

'No! If I'd known, I never would've come!'

'Will it be like this the whole way?'

'I expect so. Be quiet, Morag. I can't talk!'

Morag sank back. The nausea was unbearable. She put her arms around the tiny baby and hitched the blanket up over her head. Nothing could ever be worse than this, she thought to herself. If only we can get through this sickness, we can put up with anything.

Further down the row of berths an old man was praying out loud, his voice cracking with terror, 'Lord, we never should have left our homes!' he cried in despair.

Janet Matheson let out a long mournful wail.

'Babylon! Babylon! They're shipping us off to Babylon!'

'We're not going to Babylon, Janet!' called Morag, wanting to reassure her. 'We're only going to the new Colony in Victoria!'

But Janet took no notice. For hours her voice droned on and on.

'Babylon! Babylon! They're shipping us off to Babylon!'

Suddenly, Morag was violently sick. Sick and crying and afraid. Katie cried with her.

It was five terrible days and five worse nights before the sea-sickness began to ease. The Surgeon did his rounds each morning with the Matron beside him, giving out medicine to the most desperate cases, urging those who felt a little better to get away from the foul-smelling 'tween-decks and to go up through the hatches for some fresh air. He sent down a squad of six reluctant sailors who carried off all the over-flowing chamber pots and tin dishes and then mopped the floor of the central aisle and in between the berths. The sailors joked and sang boisterously as they worked but hardly a head was raised to look at them. Morag had long ago passed little Katie out of the bunk to Flora who carried her up to a sheltered corner of the sunny deck and spooned thin porridge into her mouth.

But an end did come at last. Though the wind blew just as strongly, though the *Georgiana* pitched and tossed and shuddered and lunged exactly as before, though the noise of running sailors, shouting officers, rattling chains and flapping sails never stopped, little by little the sickness passed and the terror lifted. Allan and Morag had found their sea-legs and they strode almost confidently along the spar deck, staring out at the blue water with its white-capped waves. One by one, their old friends and cousins emerged from below, bleary-eyed and ravenously hungry. Ewen Gordon and Allan struck up a sudden friendship and were always together. With their dark hair chopped short and their brown eyes set deep in pale faces under black eyebrows, the two boys looked almost like brothers, even like twins. Morag felt sad. She and Allan had always been so close at home but now he was drifting away from her. She looked everywhere for Rory but he was pinned to his father's side so she turned next to Kirsty and Calum. They followed her everywhere, their eyes full of admiration. They took it in turn to carry Katie for her. Kenny trailed hopefully after Allan and Ewen, wanting them to notice him. Flora made friends of her own. Morag seldom saw her now except when mealtimes came round.

Now that the sickness had passed, everyone wanted to eat. At midday the people lined the long table between the berths and waited. The captains of each mess-group walked carefully down the steps, carrying the steaming food in buckets and boxes. Allan helped his father. He lowered a box of boiled potatoes onto the table and tipped them out. Donald MacDonald put the joint of hot salty meat right down into the middle of them. Morag reached out a hand to grab a potato and she stuffed it into her mouth. Her mother pulled a piece of meat from the joint and gave it to Kenny. All along the table, at the centre of every family group, the potatoes and meat were piled up high and the people stretched out their hands and began to eat.

'No! no!' cried the Matron in tones of horror, hurrying along behind them and waving a plate in one hand and a knife and fork in the other. 'You mustn't eat like animals! Get out your plates! You were all given one when you came on board. And everyone has a knife and a fork. Get them out and I'll show you what to do!'

Jimmy ran close beside her to translate her sharp words. There was a mutter of resentment from the people but they looked under their berths and in their pockets to find the new implements that they'd forgotten all about.

The Matron demonstrated. She sat a joint of meat in the centre of a tin dish. She took a sharp knife and carved the meat into twelve thick slices. Then she set one family's plates out neatly, one in front of each person. She lifted up each potato on a fork and placed one on every plate. She dished out the slices of meat. Then, with a knife in her right hand and a fork in her left, she showed the astonished crofters how to cut the meat in front of them, how to spear each little piece, how to convey it politely to the lips. Everyone had a try, laughing and spluttering as potatoes dropped off their forks onto the floor and bits of meat shot across the table. The Matron walked up and down the rows, giving advice that no one could understand, correcting the way this child or that man held the fork, wiping her hands on her apron from time to time to clean them from the sticky hands she'd had to touch. Finally, with an exasperated sigh, she left them to it. No sooner had she gone, than the people put down their unwieldy knives and forks and picked up their food with their fingers again.

Eight days out from Greenock, the sea-sickness forgotten and their stomachs comfortably full, all the children sat about chattering with each other in large groups on the deck, the girls knitting black wool on bone needles, the boys knotting scraps of rope that the sailors had given them. Morag found it strange to be amongst so many others of her own age but it was a pleasant change. At Talisker she'd known only the four other families. As the sun shone down steadily on the ship, a little warmer and stronger with every passing day, the children pulled off their thick shawls and jackets. Morag rolled up her sleeves. She felt an unexpected kind of happiness creeping over her. She liked that sun on her skin.

6

King Neptune

'Aren't you the girl who asked me for a wee bottle of ink?' asked the Captain. He was strolling about the deck from one group of children to the next with Jimmy MacLean beside him as translator.

'Yes, sir,' said Morag, getting politely to her feet to answer him. 'But I haven't written my letter yet. I was too sick.'

'And where's your father? Donald MacDonald? And your mother? And all the other good folk from your township?'

'They're still down below, sir. Most of the mothers and fathers are there. They're too unhappy and weak to get up. They eat the meals now but then they just go back to bed.'

Morag was right. Down below on the crowded berths, the older people lay huddled under their blankets even though the sea-sickness had passed. Effie and Donald Mac-Donald were stretched out on their berths, Janet Matheson was curled up small, Mary MacAskill tossed about uncomfortably. While the children sat chatting together on the deck or played games around the lifeboats, their parents and grandparents were still gripped by the misery of leaving home and by their fear of the sea. They had closed their eyes and pulled the covers up over their ears. That's how they were when Captain Murray came down the companionway with Jimmy MacLean. Morag ran close behind them to see what would happen.

'Up on deck, everyone!' shouted the Captain cheerfully, pulling blankets off the humped bodies as he strode down between the berths. 'We're having dancing on the deck in half an hour and I want every single one of you up there to join in. I know you're fine dancers, you people from Skye! Alec Matheson's got his fiddle tuned and the Cameron brothers are ready too. Neil MacKinnon's blowing on his pipes. Come on now! Up you get!'

Jimmy could hardly keep pace with the flow of words.

'Dancing!' exclaimed Effie MacDonald, sitting up and staring at the Captain in amazement. 'What do we have to be dancing about? We keep our dancing for the happy times, sir. For our weddings and the New Year. Who'd want to dance at a funeral like this?'

'This is not a funeral!' laughed the Captain. 'I want a healthy ship. There've been too many emigrant ships dogged by sickness and death in this past year. What you need is sunshine and exercise. If you go on lying down here much longer then we really will be having funerals every day. Dancing's the only cure. Come on! Everyone up on deck! The sun's shining and we've got a steady wind behind us. What more could you ask for?'

Donald MacDonald groaned but he climbed down from his berth. All along the row, slowly and reluctantly, the people got out of bed. They tried to smooth the creases out of their stained clothes and they struggled up on deck into the sunshine, their eyes dazzled by the light.

The Captain had meant what he said about the dancing. The three fiddlers and Neil MacKinnon were waiting. Alec Matheson winked at Morag as he drew his bow across the strings. Young and old were hustled into pairs and sets all the way down the deck. The dancing began. Fast and slow, merry and stately, the legs that had never wanted to move again stepped through the familiar paces of the old dances.

They danced the Old Women's Roundabout Reel and the Reel of Tulloch, the Cockfight and the Ducks' Dance, the Great Dance of Skye and the Dance of Kisses. The sailors up aloft looked down in astonishment at the sight. Captain Murray rubbed his hands together with delight.

'That's the way!' he cried. 'Now you've got the hang of it! We'll have dancing again tonight and every night till we reach the Colony! When the weather's bad and the deck's drenched with the waves, you'll just have to dance down below between the berths and the table.'

The very next day, the English lessons began. Mr Gilby took the matter in hand himself. He assembled everyone on the spar deck and called out for those who could speak some English already. Angus MacRae was the first to step forward.

'I don't like the language,' he said to Mr Gilby in his usual sour voice. 'But I can speak it all right. I had a good teacher in Kilbeg when I was a boy.'

'Right! Any more?'

A small sandy-haired man spoke up quietly.

'I was a schoolmaster on Skye,' he said hesitantly. 'It was only a tiny school in our own black house and I had my father's croft to look after as well, you know. But I can teach the English.'

'Splendid!' said Mr Gilby. 'What's your name, man?

'Malcolm MacQueen.'

'Good. Now, any more?'

Here and there from the crowd a few more men came out to the front. Donald MacDonald didn't move. He was proud of his bit of English but he knew it wasn't enough. Then Allan leant over to Jimmy.

'I do know six or seven words in the English,' he murmured. When Jimmy had translated, Mr Gilby smiled at Allan.

'What are these words of yours, lad? Let me hear them.'

Now that it came to the point and with over three

hundred people listening to him, Allan was not so keen to speak.

'Go on, Allan!' urged Morag, poking him with her finger, proud to show off this clever brother of hers.

Allan took a big breath. He said his seven words very slowly, struggling to get his tongue round the awkward sounds.

'One, two, three, four, five, yes, no!'

He grinned in triumph as he reached the end of his list.

Morag clapped her hands.

'No, sorry, lad,' said Mr Gilby, his voice kind and his mouth still smiling. 'I don't think you're quite ready to be a teacher yet. But you've made a fine start. Now what we really need are a few of the women to come forward. The women and girls'll have to take their orders from the ladies in the Colony so they're going to have to understand English too. Come on, there must be a few of you good women who have picked up some English on Skye.'

To Morag's astonishment, it was Mistress Gordon who offered first.

'I was in service in a big house in Portree once, sir,' she said to Mr Gilby. 'I can speak the language well enough for housekeeping.'

'That's just what we want! Any more?'

Five of the younger women came out. Mr Gilby beamed at them.

'Don't worry about reading and writing,' he said. 'Just stick to talking. That's what matters in the Colony. But if anyone wants a book, you can use the Shorter Catechism. Now Jimmy, tell the people to choose the teacher they want.'

Jimmy explained. Morag, with little Katie straddling her hip, made a dash for Mistress Gordon. Flora and her mother followed quickly. Mistress Gordon may have lived in a gravel-pit for years and her voice was rough but she was kind.

'Rory! You stay here by me!' said Angus MacRae sharply when he saw Rory about to sidle off to another teacher. 'And you, boy!' he added, pointing a long finger at Allan. 'Donald MacDonald's son, I mean, and that skinny little brother of yours. I'll take both of you too. Now who else'll we have?' He looked around for more pupils to draw into his circle, starting with Ewen and Calum.

'Go off and get those English Catechisms from under your berths,' he barked, 'and we'll make a start straight away. There's no time to lose.'

Donald MacDonald joined Malcolm MacQueen's group. He liked the idea of learning from a proper schoolmaster, even if the man did seem very young. Neil MacKinnon went with him.

Thirty women and girls, along with several squawking babies, sat on the hard boards of the deck in a ring around Mistress Gordon.

'Will we learn the Catechism too?' asked Morag eagerly. 'Just like the boys?'

Mistress Gordon looked worried.

'I'm sorry, Morag. I can't *read* the English, you know. I can only speak it. I could teach you a song that Mistress Robertson used to sing to her babies.'

'Will it help us in the Colony?' asked Morag doubtfully.

'It might. You might be a nursemaid to a baby in a big family.'

'I could be a nursemaid too!' Flora butted in. 'I'm good with babies.'

'All right,' said Mistress Gordon. 'We'll start with the song.' She took Katie from Morag's arms and began to rock her gently as she sang.

> *Hush-a-bye baby, on the tree top,*
> *When the wind blows the cradle will rock,*
> *When the bough breaks, the cradle will fall,*
> *Down will come baby, cradle and all.*

'What does it mean?' asked Flora.

Mistress Gordon explained the song. All her listeners were silent.

'Those English people must be very strange,' said Morag indignantly, 'if they put their babies to sleep up in the trees! Will we have to climb the trees with their babies when we get to the Colony?'

'It's just a song they sing, Morag,' said Mistress Gordon with a smile. 'They don't really put their babies up in the trees. Now come on, you can all sing it with me.'

Mistress Gordon must have sung the song twenty times, over and over again. The women and girls couldn't seem to get the hang of it but first Flora and then Morag and Kirsty and the other girls and at last the women too began to join in with the singing. They all held invisible babies in their arms. They all rocked from side to side as they sang, laughing out loud at the mistakes they made. At the end of an hour they could sing it right through.

'That's enough for today,' said Mistress Gordon. 'Tomorrow I'll teach you what to say when the lady of the house comes to the kitchen to give you your orders for the day.'

'Come on Kirsty!' said Morag, springing to her feet. We'll find Allan and see how he got on. Perhaps he learnt a song too.'

Allan and Ewen sat glumly with Calum on the edge of a top berth. They hadn't learnt any English songs in Angus MacRae's group.

'What did you learn then?' asked Morag.

'We learnt the first question and answer in the Catechism,' said Allan and he broke into stumbling English, parroting Angus MacRae's own gloomy voice. 'What is the chief end of man? Man's chief end is to glorify God, and to enjoy Him forever.'

'Are you going to learn the whole Catechism off by heart?' asked Morag, greatly impressed.

'I think so,' Allan groaned.

'Will it be any use in the Colony?' said Kirsty.

'No! What use could it be?' said Allan angrily. 'I want to learn words about sheep and cattle but Angus MacRae says we can easily pick those things up for ourselves. He says he wants to guard us from evil.'

Morag felt glad she had Mistress Gordon for a teacher.

The *Georgiana* sailed steadily south. Dirty bedding and clothing were brought up on deck and washed and spread out to dry in the sunshine. Decks and berths were scrubbed clean with buckets of salt water and blocks of holystone. The people chanted their English lessons in sing-song choruses all along the deck every morning. To Morag's irritation, Flora was by far the quickest in Mistress Gordon's group. She seemed to have an ear for the language. Even when the lesson was over, she walked up and down by the ship's rail, reciting little conversations out loud to herself. She nodded and smiled as she talked.

' "Good morning, Flora." "Good morning, Mistress Robertson." "Today we shall make a plum pudding." "Yes, Mistress Robertson. Shall I bring the flour?" "Yes, bring the flour and bring the eggs." "Oh, Mistress Robertson, we have only one egg left!" "Then run to the henhouse and gather some more." '

'Who's this Mistress Robertson you keep talking to?' Allan asked her. 'I can't see anyone.'

'She was the lady Mistress Gordon used to work for in Portree. We have to talk to her all the time when we're learning the English.'

'That's stupid!' said Allan. 'The ladies in Victoria won't all be called Mistress Robertson!'

'It's not stupid!' said Flora. 'And I think the English is easy! I'm the best in our class!'

'Don't show off!' said Morag, taking Allan's side. 'You may be good at the English, Flora, but you'll be forgetting the Gaelic before long!'

'I never will forget it!' said Flora indignantly. 'People never forget their real language.'

'I'm not so sure,' said Morag, still amazed that a child of nine could prattle on so effortlessly about flour and eggs in the strange new tongue.

The weather grew warmer. Within a few weeks it was unbearably hot. The sailors hoisted an awning up over the deck to keep off the fiercest rays of the sun but down below in the sleeping quarters the air was stifling. The unpleasant smells were overpowering. Small sails were rigged up by the open hatches to try to catch some air and blow it down below but that made little difference. Many of the families chose to leave their berths at night and to sleep up on the open deck where they could breathe more easily. Day after day, as the blazing heat grew fiercer, the crofters' pale faces turned browner in the sun.

Morag kept a good look out for Jimmy MacLean. Whenever she saw him he was shinning up a mast or hauling on a rope or 'laying' (as he called it) over a yard or keeping his watch with Walter MacDougall. Sometimes he even took his turn at the wheel with an older seaman beside him. Jimmy seemed to be at every sailor's beck and call, mending sails with the sailmaker, sawing spars with the carpenter, scrubbing decks at daybreak, helping the burly cook, Jamie Cross, in the galley. He had a hard life, Morag thought, but he seemed to like it. She never heard him complain.

In spite of the terrible heat, the Captain kept the people at their dancing. And when they weren't dancing, they were practising their new, broken English, or knitting their scratchy, hot wool, or singing their old songs from home. The Gaelic Bibles were brought out and the better readers read aloud to circles of quiet listeners. And, at the end of each day, every father led his own family in prayer as they stood beside their berths. Time passed slowly. Morag felt she'd be on that ship forever.

Suddenly she noticed how very much better everyone was beginning to look. Those who'd been wasted with hunger had plumper cheeks and stronger arms. Katie's thin little face and bony ribs were filling out. Kirsty Gordon's grating cough had eased. Allan seemed to have grown an inch taller and his voice was starting to break. Ewen and Calum had lost their look of terror. And Rory MacRae, whenever he could escape from his father, liked to sit close to Morag and her friends in their shady corner of the deck. Angus MacRae had been given a job with the ship's carpenter so Rory was free to sit with Morag more often but he hadn't quite lost his fears. He still kept one ear cocked for his father's footsteps on the deck. Sometimes Morag would catch him looking blankly out to sea, his eyes shadowy and withdrawn.

'Rory! Whatever's the matter?' she asked him again and again but he never had an answer to give her.

More than once the ship lay becalmed and the sails hung limp and lifeless in the heat. The people grew restless and anxious. Then suddenly a new wind would spring up. The drooping sails began to fill, the sailors were shouting and running and the ship was moving forwards again with bright shoals of flying fish soaring in her wake. 'Cheerily men!' sang the sailors as they hauled on the sheets and spread more sail. The mood of gloom all over the ship lifted with the billowing canvas.

One day, Jimmy stopped to talk with Morag.

'I've got something to tell you,' he whispered.

'What is it?' asked Morag eagerly.

'It's about the gold!' said Jimmy, grinning at her in excitement.

'I know! The sailors want to run off to the diggings!'

Jimmy gazed at her, astonished.

'How did you guess?'

'I heard two of them talking on the day we left Greenock.

Walter MacDougall and John MacNeill. Are you going with them, Jimmy?'

'I don't know what to do,' he said. 'They've asked me to join them. I want to find gold. Who wouldn't? But I love this ship, Morag. If I run off with the others, Captain Murray's not likely to take me back again, is he?'

'You could ask him if he'd let you go,' she suggested. 'Just for a month while the ship's in port. Then you'd come back again.'

'But the men don't want me to mention the gold to the Captain. Not a word about gold! That's what Jamie Cross said. Their plan's a secret.'

Morag felt sorry for Jimmy. He looked so worried.

'Will we be much longer on this ship of yours?' she asked him. 'Are we nearly there?'

'No, not nearly! This voyage lasts three months!'

'But won't we be stopping at a port somewhere? Some place where we can walk off the ship and stretch our legs?'

Jimmy shook his head.

'No ports-of-call. Some ships stop at Cape Town, but not this one. We've got stores and water to last us the whole way to Geelong. But we're almost at the Line now.' Jimmy was his cheerful self again.

'What Line?' asked Morag.

'The Equator. We call it the Line. It's a line right round the world. It's hotter there than anywhere else.'

Morag looked out over the sparkling water.

'I can't see any Line,' she said.

'No one can see it. It's invisible. But I've seen it on a map. The Captain himself showed me.'

Morag was disappointed. What was the use of a Line if no one could see it.

'When we cross the Line, King Neptune's coming on board,' Jimmy went on. 'He'll climb up near the fo'c'sle. There'll be fun and games for the sailors when he comes and I'll probably get the worst of it!'

'Why you?'

'Because I've never crossed the Line before.'

'Is he really a King?' she asked him, still puzzled.

'Of course he is! King of the Ocean! King of the Sea!'

'I've never heard of him, Jimmy.'

'Then there's a lot you haven't heard of! Everyone else knows about King Neptune.'

But when Morag asked among her friends and relations she found that none of them knew any more about King Neptune that she did. Her father was quite indignant.

'King of the Ocean!' he exclaimed. 'That's a lot of nonsense, Morag! There's only one King of the Ocean and that's the Lord God himself. This Neptune person sounds like an impostor to me.'

Late that same afternoon, the ship's clanging bell welcomed King Neptune on board. The crofters crowded forward to watch the short, stout man as he clambered up over the side of the ship in his flowing robes. He had a tawdry crown on his head, a trident in one hand and a smile on his broad, bearded face. He waved. A bunch of ragged courtiers clustered close around him. Jimmy was the first sailor they grabbed. Helpless with laughter, he was bound hand and foot and 'shaved' with a fearsome long razor and much brushing of foaming white lather and dirty, black tar at the end of a broom. He didn't protest even when the King ordered him to be dumped three times in a tub of salt water. Morag was horrified.

'What a cruel King!' she murmured to her mother. 'And Jimmy had hardly any whiskers to be shaved off anyway. I hope the King's not going to start on Father next.'

Everyone had the same fear. The men fingered their beards nervously. But the Captain appeared suddenly beside the King and assured them that Neptune came only to trouble the seamen. No one else would be plunged into the water. Angus MacRae was not satisfied by that.

'It's wicked!' he shouted from the back of the crowd.

'No one should be watching it. Rory, come here at once and get below!' And he dragged the unwilling Rory down to the darkness of the berths.

The Captain simply shrugged his shoulders and the King went on with his antics. Morag's father was almost as disapproving as Angus MacRae at first but he couldn't help staying to watch. Before long he was laughing with the rest of them. When the last new sailor had been shaved, the King and his followers disappeared again over the side of the ship.

'Is he really a King?' asked Morag, still bewildered.

'It's only a sailor dressed up!' shouted Allan, very pleased with himself. At the very last minute he had recognized Jamie Cross, the cook, under the golden paper crown.

'I knew that all the time,' pretended Morag quickly, her face red.

Everyone was laughing. The frightened children had stopped their wailing and Alec Matheson was tuning up his fiddle. Soon it would be time to dance again.

7

The Roaring Forties

'Sail Ho!'

The cry rang out from the crow's-nest, high aloft.

Everyone rushed to the port rail to look out over the water at the faint white mark on the horizon that slowly grew into a sail and then into a fully-rigged ship. It was the first vessel they'd seen for weeks. She was sailing north-east as they sailed south-west. Would she come close enough for the Captain to hail her? Would they see any people aboard her? Would she take letters home for them? Everyone on the *Georgiana* felt the same strange longing for the sight of other people in the middle of that vast and empty ocean.

The two ships drew closer. They faced each other, swaying and dipping in the water like partners in a dance. To a chorus of shouting and singing, the seamen hauled on the sheets and swarmed up into the rigging of both ships to take in the sails. The forward motion was suddenly checked. Morag was astonished to see how deeply the prow of the other ship plunged and how high it reared up again, even though the sea was calm. She had grown so used to the pitching of her own ship that she hardly noticed it now. The Captain of the *Georgiana* hailed the newcomer through a speaking-trumpet.

'Ship ahoy!' he called.

'Hullo!' came the faint answer from a figure on the other ship.

8

'What ship is that, pray?'

'*Clarinda*.'

'Where are you from?'

'Cape Town.'

'Where are you bound?'

'For London. What is your ship, pray?'

'*Georgiana* from Greenock. Bound for Geelong. Will you take letters?'

'Yes. Gladly. We sail on in two hours.'

'Thank you, *Clarinda*!' shouted the Captain, and lowered his trumpet.

An excited flurry of letter-writing began at once. Mr Gilby sent Jimmy around the decks with small sheets of paper and a bunch of pencils. Anyone who could write at all set to work to speak with those they'd left at home. Most of the women and many of the men couldn't write and they had to find someone else to put a few brief words onto paper for them. Morag wrote in Gaelic to the minister at Carbost, dipping her sharp new pen in the bottle of ink. She told him about Greenock and Katie, about the sea-sickness, about Jimmy and King Neptune, about Rory and his disagreeable father, about the English lessons and the dancing under the stars.

And we read the Bible every day, she added quickly, in case the minister might think there was far too much frivolity on board, *and we sing the Psalms. And every Sabbath morning one of the men preaches a sermon but Father says they are not nearly as good as yours. He says your sermons always had the root of the matter in them.*

Mother helps to milk the cows in their little pen on the deck. She says their skin is so smooth against her cheek and they give much more milk every day than our dear old Peggy ever did at home. If you walk over to Talisker, Mr Cameron, would you please see that little Peggy is doing fine? I miss her so much and I liked her rough coat. And if you ever go right down to the shore

79

at Talisker, would you see if the purple sea-thrift is flowering well this year? I often think about it and I wonder if there'll be any flowers in the new country?

The time passes so slowly on this ship, Mr Cameron. I'm sometimes afraid we'll never get there. And the sailors tell us such frightening tales about the Colony — about wild animals and terrible fires and raging floods. Jimmy translates everything they say. Most of all, they talk about the gold. Father says gold does not matter but I'd like to find just one enormous nugget. Then we could all sail home to Skye again.

Within two hours the letters were finished, folded, addressed and sealed with red wax. Precious pennies were paid out to Mr Gilby for the stamps. The whole bundle of letters was wrapped in a piece of strong waterproof cloth and ferried across to *Clarinda* in the smallest boat. Every eye watched anxiously as the bundle was hoisted on board the other ship. A cheer of relief rang out. The emigrants gazed at the unknown people who lined the rail of the *Clarinda* and those people gazed back at them with the same fascination. Then the great sails were spread again and the two ships moved apart.

There was no dancing on the deck that night. No one quite had the heart for it. Writing those letters home had brought back all the sadness of leaving Skye. Even the next day the crofters gave only half their attention to the English lessons. They kept thinking of the *Clarinda* as she sailed north to London with their bundle of letters on board for the folk at home on Skye. The sailors too were subdued.

Three days later they sighted the island of Fernando de Noronha, off the coast of Brazil. Great white birds flew out from the shore to the ship as the green land came closer. Morag was hoping that perhaps the *Georgiana* would sail into a quiet harbour where they could all walk about on solid ground again. But with a sudden burst of shouts from the Captain and answering cries from the seamen on the sheets below and on the yards above, the ship changed course dramatically and swung from the south-west to the south-east. Away from the island.

'Why are we going this way?' she asked Jimmy who was running past her in answer to the Bosun's shrill whistle.

He barely paused to speak.

'We always follow the currents and the winds,' he panted. 'Now we'll be picking up the trade winds that'll take us far to the south of Cape Town. Then we'll find the west winds – the Roaring Forties. We won't see land again till we reach the Colony. But we might see icebergs and whales!'

The Bosun's whistle blew again and Jimmy ran off. Morag looked back at the slowly-vanishing island. That night, lying out on the deck and trying to sleep as the ship ploughed steadily south and east, she noticed how different the stars had become in the past few weeks. The Great Bear and the North Star had disappeared below the horizon and along with them had gone most of the old familiar constellations she'd known on Skye. Now a bright new group of stars like a blazing white cross hung high above them in the blackness. The Milky Way was thicker with stars than she'd ever seen it in the misty north. She felt she really had left the old world behind her now. They were sailing into an utterly new world where even the heavens above them were strange. Only the moon by night and the sun by day were still their faithful companions as the last of the land-birds dropped behind.

Now the winds blew colder. The awning came down again as the sun shone less fiercely. The shawls and the warm jackets were brought out from under the berths. The English lessons moved down below to the long table between the bunks. Lime-juice had been added to the weekly rations, bitter and sharp on the tongue.

'What's it for?' Morag asked Jimmy as he poured the green liquid into everyone's pannikin.

'It's to stop us all getting sick with scurvy,' he said.

Morag swallowed her lime-juice with a shudder.

'Jimmy,' she said, lowering her voice. 'Have you decided what to do yet? About running off to the diggings with the other sailors to look for gold?'

Jimmy's blue eyes glanced out at the sea and then turned back to Morag.

'I'm not going to run off,' he said quietly. 'I've made up my mind. I've told Jamie Cross. He's not too pleased with me. He keeps trying to scare me into joining them and he makes threats in the fo'c'sle at night.'

'What sort of threats?'

'He says they've got knives. Long knives and guns. He says he'll slit my throat if I breathe a word to the Captain.'

'Jimmy!' gasped Morag.

'He might just be bluffing. I haven't ever seen these long knives he keeps talking about. But I do get scared all the same. I'd never tell the Captain. And don't you tell anyone either, Morag, or we might both get our throats slit!'

'I won't!' said Morag, suddenly cold and frightened.

'Jamie Cross says all the ships at Geelong and Melbourne are deserted now. The whole Colony's gone mad with gold-fever. Captain Murray won't be able to hold the men on this ship. But he'll hold on to me all right. I love this ship of his.'

'I wish *I* could go to the diggings, Jimmy,' said Morag. 'With Allan, I mean, or with you. We'd be sure to pick up a nugget somewhere.'

Jimmy was horrified.

'The diggings are no place for a girl, Morag! They're wild places. Dangerous places. Anyway, Jamie Cross says there aren't any nuggets to be found on the ground nowadays. It's all digging, digging, digging. With the sun blazing down on your back and the flies buzzing round your head and the snakes crawling into your blankets. You mustn't think of going there! It wouldn't be safe.'

'But . . .' began Morag.

'Man overboard!' came a sudden cry from the main mast, high above their heads.

Jimmy sprang forward and then aft. Morag grabbed the rail and looked out over the sea. She could see nothing but the swirl of green water and the white heaving waves.

Sailors were running and shouting. Two small children were screaming and pointing. Morag's eyes followed the line of their fingers.

Then she saw. It was not a man overboard. It was a woman. A woman who'd climbed onto a lifeboat to peg out her washing on a line she'd rigged up for herself. A fierce blast of wind must have lifted her bodily into the air and thrown her right into the sea. There she was now, wallowing helplessly in the water, her skirts puffed up with air and keeping her just afloat. The sailors flung a rope but she couldn't reach it. They hurled themselves on the sheets to reduce sail and slow the ship but already the woman was being left behind.

'Lower the boat!' shouted the Captain.

By the time the ship had hove to in the mounting waves and the boat had been lowered, it was too late. The woman had gone.

Morag watched the whole thing in horror. She felt paralysed with shock. The terrible cry and the shouting of the sailors had brought all the crofters running up on deck. They packed close together along the rail and stared unbelievingly at the water where the woman had been floundering and calling for help not a minute before.

'Who is it? Who was it? What's happened?' Morag heard them asking one another. The answer came soon enough. Everyone was talking.

'It's Mistress Nicolson.'

'Anna Nicolson from Glenmore?'

'Yes, that's the one.'

'She's the wife of Alasdair Nicolson.'

'Where are the children? She has two of them. Two little girls.'

'Look, there they are. Crying, poor things, and no wonder.'

Alasdair Nicolson himself came staggering through the crowd as the grim news reached him. He rushed to his children and wrapped his arms around them. They huddled together, still looking down at the water, even though the boat had been pulled back on board and the ship had spread her sails again and was picking up speed.

Captain Murray came at once to try to comfort the man. Mr Gilby came too but Alasdair Nicolson pushed them away.

'You should have saved her!' he shouted at them. His face blazed with anger. 'You were too slow! She was a good woman! All she was doing was hanging up the washing! She's gone! My Anna! She's gone!'

Urging the two bewildered children along in front of him, he stumbled below and threw himself onto his berth. He lay there sobbing for hours and his children sobbed beside him. All through the night his crying went on in the darkness. His children slept with exhaustion. Everyone on the other bunks joined in his tears and wailing. It was a wake without a body. A mourning without a funeral. Mr Gilby tried to calm them, walking from berth to berth with a lantern in his hand, speaking awkward words of comfort, but only the next morning did the crying stop long enough for the Captain to read the burial service for Anna Nicolson.

Mistress Gordon spoke to the grief-crazed man when he was back on his berth again, a whimpering child each side of him.

'I could help you with the children if you'll let me,' she said, her rough voice softer. 'They'll be needing some food.'

Alasdair Nicolson sat up and stared at her, not understanding at first. Then he nodded.

'Take them for a while. They're fond of your daughter, Kirsty.'

The two small girls climbed from the berth and followed Mistress Gordon. Their eyes were glazed. Alasdair Nicolson lay down and pulled the blanket up over his head. He groaned in despair.

Hundreds of miles to the south of the Cape, right on the Fortieth parallel, the *Georgiana* swung to the east as the Roaring Forties filled her sails and hurtled her through the sea. Within two days Morag realized that even the roughest weather on the voyage so far had been nothing compared with this. The wind blew to a gale, the gale to a storm, the storm to a hurricane. The people were sent below and the hatches were battened down. Enormous waves broke over the deck above their heads, crashing and roaring as they fell. The ship rolled so far to port and then so far to starboard that she lay for a few terrible seconds every time, almost on her side. She shuddered and her timbers groaned with the strain. Two great waterbutts broke loose on the upper deck and rolled from one side to the other with a noise like thunder. The mainsail split with a crack. The mizzen top-mast snapped. Seamen ran and shouted in answer to the Mate's bellowed orders. The helmsman was lashed to the wheel and Captain Murray himself stood beside him, tied to a stanchion so no wave could snatch him away.

Morag was frightened. Everyone was frightened. Terrified. They all lay stretched on their berths as the lamps swung violently and the sea and wind howled around them. Water poured in through the closed hatches and even seeped through the cracks between the boards. The bedding was soaked and the floors were awash. Voices were crying. Morag kept thinking of what it would be like when the torrent of green water finally filled the whole ship. She imagined the *Georgiana* drifting slowly downwards to the sand and rocks far below. She closed her fingers on the small white shell in her pocket – the shell from the Isle of Skye.

'Shell!' she whispered. 'Shell of the sea! Speak to the wind and make it stop blowing! Speak to the waves and make them lie still!'

It was at this worst moment of fear in the storm that Morag heard Mary MacAskill's terrible groan from the berth beside her. It was a sound quite different from all the crying and sobbing around them.

'Effie!' Mary called urgently. 'Come down and help me! Be quick!'

'What is it?' asked Morag as her mother slid out of her bunk without a word.

'The baby's coming!' gasped Mary and she groaned again.

'Lie down, Morag!' said her mother sharply over her shoulder. 'This is not for you to be watching.'

But Morag didn't lie down. She wriggled to the edge of her berth and gazed across the narrow gap in fascination at the little she could manage to see in that shadowy tilting world. It was a short but painful labour. Mary MacAskill stretched her hands above her head to grasp two upright posts at the end of the bed. As she grasped, she groaned. Morag's mother held hard to Mary's bent leg on one side. Janet Matheson held her leg hard on the other side. As the ship rolled far to starboard and hung there for a long trembling moment as if it would never right itself again, Mary gave one last loud groan, the two women strained against her legs and the sixth MacAskill baby shot into the world. Its little cry joined all the clamour of the wind and sea.

While Morag's mother tied and cut the cord and wrapped the new baby girl snugly in a clean sheet and waited for the after-birth to come, Janet wiped Mary's face gently and gave her cold water to sip from a mug. Throughout it all, Donald MacAskill had sat calmly at the head of the bunk above his wife's, never looking down, his legs hanging over the side. He was trying to read his Bible in the feeble, moving light and trying to protect the Good Book from the water that dripped in from above. He glanced below for an instant and saw Morag still staring in shock and wonder at the scene of the birth.

'We're in God's hands, Morag,' he said to her. 'Lie down and sleep now.'

She was too exhausted and astonished from all she had seen to answer him. She lay and slept.

The storm raged on for four days and four nights. It seemed to Morag an eternity of terror. But on the fourth morning she watched in joy as the hatches were opened from above and a sickly beam of sunshine crept in. The ship was no longer rolling or pitching. The wind had dropped. As the people struggled up on deck, their legs weak and shaking, they found the crew of drenched and weary sailors already hoisting fresh sails, erecting a newly-mended top-mast, setting to rights the chaos that the storm had brought. But all the cows had gone. They'd been swept overboard. For the rest of the journey there'd be no fresh milk for the children. They'd just have to make do with oatmeal soaked in water. Effie MacDonald grieved for those cows.

As the sun shone more strongly and the sea turned blue again, the ship in her new sails skimmed merrily along over the water, and the wet bedding, spread out on deck, began to dry. The Captain called the emigrants together and asked one of the older men from Skye to offer thanks to God for their deliverance. Never had their prayers been more heartfelt. It seemed to them a sheer miracle that they were still alive to breathe the air and see the sky. They felt like Jonah, sicked up from the belly of the whale, standing unsteadily on his feet at last.

Then the Captain took the new MacAskill baby in his arms and poured three cupfuls of salt water over her head.

'Georgiana,' he said solemnly. 'I baptize thee in the name of the Father and of the Son and of the Holy Ghost.'

Morag wondered why she was crying all of a sudden. There was really nothing to cry about now. They were safe from the storm. The tiny baby was thriving.

'There's never been a child on Skye called Georgiana!' muttered Angus MacRae in irritation to anyone who would listen to him. 'It's not a Skye name at all. Why can't they give the girl a proper name like Kirsty or Catriona or Flora?'

'It's because of the ship,' said Morag, wiping her eyes. 'And because of the storm.'

But Angus MacRae still didn't seem to understand and he shook his head with disapproval.

As the last weeks of the voyage slipped by, Morag saw no icebergs at all and only the distant spouting of a whale. With a fine steady wind blowing from behind and a cold clear sky above, the ship raced due east towards Bass Strait and Port Phillip Bay and the port of Geelong. A wandering albatross followed close behind them now. Morag and her friends sat for hours in the stern, their eyes fixed in fascination on the barely-moving wings of the great bird. From all over the ship came the sounds of other children playing their old familiar games from Skye – hopping along the deck, skipping with an odd piece of rope, hiding behind bulkheads and lifeboats, laughing and calling. The storm was forgotten.

On Thursday the 7th October, eighty-six days out from Greenock and only a few days before the ship was expected to reach the end of her voyage, Morag came across Jimmy on the quarter deck. He had his back to her. He was busy coiling a length of new rope, his brown hands moving steadily.

'Jimmy!' she called.

He turned towards her. Morag gasped. His left eye was swollen and black. His cheek was cut and bruised.

'Whatever's happened?' she asked.

'Jamie Cross hit me,' he mumbled, making sure no one else was within earshot. 'It's all that trouble about the gold again. Last night he said I had to join the rest of the crew when they all run off in Geelong. I said I wouldn't so he punched me in the eye. He's afraid I'll tell the Captain about their plans but I wouldn't do that, Morag! You believe me, don't you?'

Morag nodded. She felt frightened for Jimmy. Whatever would those seamen do to him next? She almost wished he'd agree to join their planned escape. Perhaps he'd be safer that way. But she knew he'd never leave his ship.

'Jimmy MacLean!' came the Bosun's shout from close beside them. 'Stop your gossiping and get on with that rope!'

Morag moved quickly away.

As the *Georgiana* came nearer to Geelong, the crofters were busy gathering their belongings together, packing and repacking their bundles and boxes. The foot-ploughs and the spinning-wheels were brought up from the hold and propped against the ends of the berths where everyone tripped over them. Donald MacDonald had taken down his pouch from its hook and fixed it to the belt at his waist again. He pushed his hand into it time and time again, letting the black earth from Talisker run through his fingers. The closer he came to the new country, the more he wanted to hold onto the old. Allan and Ewen spent hours leaning over the rail of the ship, hoping to be the first to spy land. But there was still nothing to be seen except the rolling ocean and the wide blue sky. Australia was somewhere out there to the north of them, so the sailors said.

Morag had been lugging little Katie around on her hip for most of the voyage, passing her over to Flora or Kirsty when she was tired, taking it in turns with her mother to feed her with porridge. Katie crawled everywhere when

Morag put her down. Now suddenly, in the space of a few days, she was starting to walk. First she stood up, swaying and smiling, holding onto one of Morag's hands and one of Flora's. Then she took a few unsteady steps, still gripping tight. Then one morning she simply let go and staggered forwards, crowing with triumph and delight as she lurched alone across the rolling deck.

'Katie! You're walking!' shouted Morag in amazement and ran to hug her. 'You're the cleverest little sister in all the world!'

'She's not a sister,' said Flora crossly. 'She's only a cousin.'

'It's much the same,' said Morag. 'She's part of our family.'

'Well, she's not really very clever. She might be starting to walk but she can't talk English yet. She can't talk at all. I'm the best on this ship at English! I'm much better than you, Morag MacDonald!'

Morag didn't answer. She knew it was true. Somehow those hard English words flowed off Flora's tongue like water from a spring. She lifted Katie up to her hip again and walked slowly around the deck, singing one of the old songs. The words comforted her as she sang.

> *Ho ro, my baby, ho ro,*
> *You are the child of the swan,*
> *Ho ro, ho ro.*
>
> *Ho ro, my baby, ho ro,*
> *The swan left you there by the loch,*
> *Ho ro, ho ro.*
>
> *Ho ro, my baby, ho ro,*
> *I brought you safe to my house,*
> *Ho ro, ho ro.*
>
> *Ho ro, my baby, ho ro,*
> *The swan will come searching for you,*
> *Ho ro, ho ro.*

Ho ro, my baby, ho ro,
She'll search by the loch and the shore,
Ho ro, ho ro.

Ho ro, my baby, ho ro,
The swan will go flying away,
Ho ro, ho ro.

Ho ro, my baby, ho ro,
Forget the swan's feathers and feet,
Ho ro, ho ro.

Ho ro, my baby, ho ro,
You are safe in my arms, little swan,
Ho ro, ho ro.

'That's a fine song you're singing, Morag,' Alec Matheson called to her from his favourite warm spot on the deck. 'And where did you learn it?' He had his fiddle out from its cloth and he was tuning the strings.

'From my grandma at Borlin,' she said proudly.

'I remember your grandma well,' said Alec. 'I even knew her old mother too, you know. You're a bit like both of them as a matter of fact. The same dark hair. The same kind face. The same clear voice.'

Morag smiled.

'Did you know we're having a ceilidh here tonight?' Alec asked her, his eyes dancing in excitement. 'You'll be needing your warmest clothes and a blanket too. We'll have songs and stories all night long till the sun comes up in the morning. You could sing that song of yours, Morag. The song about the swan.'

'But what will my father say?' said Morag anxiously. 'And Angus MacRae? My father's troubled by those old stories and Angus really hates them.'

'Don't you be worrying about that, Morag girl. I've had a word with the Captain. He'll be speaking with them both. He says there's nothing wrong at all with the stories so long as we just remember they're not true.'

'But they *are* true, Alec! My grandma told me!'

'You're right, Morag, but don't be saying one word about it. The old tales are true, of course they are, but we'll keep that a secret. And tonight we'll have three hundred people and more sitting around our fire to listen to the stories again.'

'But we can't have a fire! Not on the deck of a ship!'

'Just you wait and see!' said Alec.

'Come on, my little Katie!' shouted Morag happily. 'When the moon rises tonight, you'll be sitting by a fire! You'll be hearing the old stories for the very first time!'

Katie gurgled and laughed.

Behind the *Georgiana*, the albatross still flew steadily onwards, keeping the ship company right to the journey's end.

8

Telling the Old Tales

As the full moon rose, all the emigrants crowded up onto
the quarter deck and found a place to sit. When Morag
first saw the fire, she was disappointed. It was nothing like
the peat fires on Skye. The cook had lent one of his smaller
stoves and the carpenter had bolted it to the deck so it
wouldn't slip about as the ship rolled. The fire of coal and
wood sent out a warm glow on the side where the stove
doors were open wide. Morag wanted to make sure her
family sat on that side.

The Captain himself was there already with Mr Gilby,
sitting on two chairs by the starboard rail and looking down
on the excited crofters as they clustered around the fire.
Captain Murray seemed to have persuaded Morag's father
and even Angus MacRae that there was nothing really
wrong with the old songs and stories. Everyone was
there.

'Just as long as you remember that not a word of them
is true, Morag!' said her father as they took their place on
the deck.

'I'll remember, Father,' she said meekly, but smiling to
herself.

Rory had managed to give his father the slip. He sat
close to Morag in the front row but Angus MacRae himself
chose the very back of the crowd, in the shadows. Alec
Matheson began the evening with a few merry tunes on

his fiddle. Then came the singing. Morag sang about the child of the swan and Effie MacDonald beamed with pride.

Janet Matheson launched into the first story. Hers was a long sad tale about the water-horse who came out of the Talisker River and snatched three children away. Though their mothers wept for years, the children never returned. When Janet reached the end of her tale there was a burst of clapping and a gasp of fear.

'Of course,' Donald broke in loudly, 'there never were any water-horses on Skye, you know.'

Everyone nodded solemnly and waited impatiently for the next story to begin. It was not long in coming.

There were stories of witches – the wicked kind and the good – and of the fairies who live underground. There were stories of babies taken from their cradles and of the disagreeable changelings who were left in their place. Morag liked best the tale of a crofter who stole a gravestone to use in a wall. The ghost of the man who'd been buried under that stone haunted him every night till he put it back on the grave. Then there was the story of the piper who vanished into a fairy cave and another about the woman who saw a funeral procession coming up the road just a week before her husband died.

Rory sat enthralled. He'd never heard any of these tales before. Morag loved to glance at his astonished face in the firelight. Then to her amazement she heard her father himself offering to tell a story.

'Of course, not a word of it's true!' he said. 'My poor old father was an ignorant man. He used to say that this really happened to his own father and his uncle down on Loch Scavaig. But that can't be true at all. It's only a story.'

'Go on, Donald man!' urged Alec Matheson. 'Just tell us your tale!'

'Right,' said Donald MacDonald, his whole face and voice changing as he began his story. 'I'll tell you the tale of Black Donald and Fair Donald.'

94

Once upon a time, long long ago, there lived two brothers. They were fishermen. One of these brothers had dark hair so he was known as Black Donald. The other brother had yellow hair, so he was known as Fair Donald. They lived in a little black hut on the edge of the great sea-loch.

One dark night in the middle of winter, when the brothers were sitting by the fire and mending their nets, a terrible storm blew up. The wind raged and the thunder roared. The lightning flashed and the rain beat down against the roof of the hut. The brothers drew closer to the fire and stirred their pot of porridge.

'Brother! Do you hear that noise,' cried Black Donald suddenly, starting up from his stool.

'I hear the wind and the rain,' said Fair Donald.

'No! There's another sound out there in the storm! Listen!'

Fair Donald listened. Very faintly, under the roar of the wind, came a timid little cry.

'Miaou! Miaou! Miaou!'

Fair Donald leapt to his feet.

'It's a poor little cat out there in the rain! Quick! We must open the door.'

They opened the door just a tiny wee crack. There on the step sat a little black cat. She was shivering with cold and drenched with rain.

'Miaou! Miaou! Miaou!' she cried.

'Come in, come in, little cat!' cried Black Donald as he flung the door wide. 'You must sit by our fire!'

'Come in, come in, little cat!' cried Fair Donald and he ran for a towel.

The little black cat hobbled in through the door. Water streamed down from her coat to the earth of the floor. Fair Donald rubbed her fur dry with his towel. Black Donald poured milk into a dish and he set it down close to the fire.

'Drink up, drink up, little cat, and stay by our fire,' he said.

Lap, lap, lap went the little black cat till all the milk was gone. Purr, purr, purr went the little black cat. She curled up by the fire and she fell fast asleep.

Early next morning, the storm had passed. A bright red sun was shining in the sky. The little black cat opened her eyes and she stretched herself by the fire. She lapped and lapped at a fresh dish of milk. Then she stood by the door and rubbed her fur against the wall. She purred and she purred.

'So you want to go out, little cat!' cried Black Donald.

He opened the door. The little black cat ran out. She scampered away across the heather to the moor and she never came back.

Now, many months later, on a fine sunny day, Black Donald and Fair Donald rowed out across the loch in their boat. By late afternoon their nets were full and they were just turning for home when a terrible storm sprang up. The sky grew dark and the wind blew hard. The rain poured down and the thunder roared. The lightning flashed and the waves mounted high. Their boat was tossed this way and that. They were driven closer and closer to the rocks on the far side of the loch. The brothers were terrified.

'We'll both be drowned!' cried Black Donald.

At that very moment, a huge wave lifted the boat high up into the air and tossed it onto the rocks by the shore. The boat was smashed to smithereens but the two brothers were safe. Bruised and bleeding, wet and cold, they staggered along the sand.

'Brother, where are we?' cried Fair Donald.

They gazed around them in the darkness and the rain. They were frightened.

'There's a light!' cried Black Donald, pointing through the night.

The two brothers stumbled on till at last they came to the light. It was shining from the window of a small black hut. They knocked on the door.

Knock, knock, knock!

'Who's there?' came a small frightened voice.

'Black Donald and Fair Donald from over the loch!' cried Black Donald. 'We've lost our boat and we're drenched with rain. Please let us in to sit by your fire!'

Now the door was opened wide and there stood a bent old woman. Her hair was white and it hung to her knees. Her long bony fingers beckoned them in. She was smiling a strange, strange smile.

'Come in, Black Donald! Come in, Fair Donald! Come in and sit by my fire. There's porridge in the pot and a bed in the wall! Come in! Come in!'

Black Donald and Fair Donald walked into the hut. They rubbed themselves dry on a clean white towel. They put on warm clothes that the old woman gave them. They sat by her fire and they ate the hot porridge. Then they climbed into the bed and they fell fast asleep.

Early next morning, the storm had passed. A bright red sun was shining in the sky. The two brothers climbed down from their bed in the wall. They sat by the fire and ate up their porridge.

'How can we thank you, Mistress, for all you have done for us?' said Black Donald to the bent old woman. 'You took us in from the storm and you gave us food and fire and bed.'

The old woman smiled her strange, strange smile.

'There's no need to thank me at all, Black Donald,' she said. 'When I was cold in the storm, you welcomed me in. When I was hungry, you gave me milk. When I was tired, you gave me a bed by your fire.'

The two brothers stared at the little old woman.

'But Mistress, we've never seen you in our lives before!' said Fair Donald. 'When did you come to our house and eat our food and sleep by our fire?'

The little old woman gave a loud long laugh and she flung the door open wide. She stepped into the bright light of day.

'I am the Witch-Cat!' she cried.

And when the brothers came out of the hut, that bent old woman was nowhere to be seen. But far over the heather they saw a little black cat, running and jumping in the sunshine.

When Donald MacDonald had finished his story, the crowd burst into cheers.

'That's the best tale of all!' cried Janet Matheson.

The night was almost over. The sky was growing light.

'We've time for one last tale and then we'll get some sleep,' said Alec.

There was a long pause.

'I'll tell you a story,' said a sour voice from the back of the crowd.

'I never thought your father would tell a story!' whispered Morag to Rory. Rory's face was pale with fear.

'Go ahead, Angus,' said Donald MacDonald.

Angus began.

Five years ago, near the little township of Kilbeg, there lived a good man with his wife and four children. The eldest child was a boy just ten years old. They lived in a black house on the edge of the sea. The good man was a carpenter and he had a small croft for growing his potatoes and for grazing his cow. But the times were very hard, as you'll all remember. There was no work for the man in Kilbeg. The blight had killed the potatoes. There were no more shellfish along the shore. So one day he decided to walk to Portree to ask for work. If only someone in Portree needed a carpenter for a week or two, he could earn a few shillings and buy food for his family.

'I'll be back when I can, Margaret,' he said, 'and I'll bring a fine bag of oats back with me. In the meantime you must drink the milk from our cow and eat the wild nettles from our croft.'

A week after the good man had left home, the eldest boy grew tired of eating nettles and drinking milk. He felt hungry. He wanted some meat in his stomach. So without saying a word to his mother, he walked up over the moor till he came to Lord MacDonald's great new flock of sheep. The shepherds were nowhere to be seen. The boy grabbed a young ewe and hoisted her onto his back. He walked home over the moors. When he came to the black house he took a sharp knife and he killed the ewe. Then he called his mother and she came to look at the wicked deed he'd done.

At first his mother was angry with the boy.

'You've stolen a sheep from the Lord MacDonald!' she cried. 'You've killed it with the knife! What will your good father say?'

But the boy told his mother what a wonderful meal they could have from that sheep. He lay on the ground and he rolled about, crying out that he was dying from hunger. The three younger children cried too. At last the mother gave in. She took the dead sheep. She skinned it and she cleaned it and she cut it into joints. She piled more peat onto the fire and she roasted the mutton. Then they all sat in a circle around the fire, gorging themselves on the stolen meat.

Just as they were nearing the end of the feast, their hands and mouths covered with grease, they heard a sound at the door. It was the good father! They started up in terror as he came into the hut.

'What's this?' roared the good man to his trembling wife. 'Mutton? Where did it come from, woman?'

She couldn't answer him. Tears of shame ran down her face.

Then the wicked boy spoke up.

'Father, we were starving with hunger!' he said. 'I stole the sheep. I brought it home and I killed it. I begged my mother to skin it and cook it. Did you want us to die?'

The good father turned to look at his wife.

'They were hungry,' she sobbed.

'You're a wicked woman!' he cried. 'You'll be punished! And that wicked boy of yours will be punished too! Come, take your shawl and bring the children. We're going back to Portree!'

'To Portree? At this time of night?' said his wife. 'The little children could never walk so far!'

'Hurry up!' said the good father. 'Justice must be done!'

The man led his family out into the night and over the long road he'd just travelled from Portree. No one spoke for the whole journey but the mother cried with shame at the wicked deed she had done.

Late in the morning they came to Portree. The good father knocked on the door of the Sheriff's officer.

'I have brought you my wife,' he said, 'and I've brought you my son. This wicked boy stole a ewe from the Lord MacDonald *and he killed it. My wife skinned it and she cooked it. All my family ate the stolen meat. They must be punished. The Commandment says plainly, "Thou shalt not steal".'*

The Sheriff's officer arrested the mother and the wicked boy. They were brought to trial and the mother was found guilty. She was transported to Van Diemen's Land and she took the three youngest children with her. The good father has never heard a word from her since. The wicked boy was pardoned because he was young. That was a mistake! The terrible guilt will haunt that boy till the end of his life!

Angus MacRae had finished his story. No one spoke. No one clapped or cheered. The tale had left a bitter taste behind it. Morag turned to look at Rory. His head was slumped forward on his chest and his eyes were shut tight. He was sobbing and the tears rolled down his cheeks. Morag put out one hand to touch him. He opened his eyes.

'I'm the wicked boy!' he whispered. 'We're going to Van Diemen's Land to find my mother and the little ones. It's all my fault that she was transported! I was the one who stole the sheep but she got all the blame.'

Morag put her arms around Rory and she hugged him.

'I don't think you're wicked!' she whispered back to him. 'I like you!'

Rory looked at Morag with astonished eyes.

'Land ahoy!' came a great cry from the crow's nest. It was Jimmy up there, keeping watch through the night.

Every head was turned to the north, and there, sure enough, just as the sun was rising, the crofters saw a faint blue smudge on the horizon and a tiny pinprick of light.

'It's the Colony!' shouted Allan, jumping up and running to the rail with Ewen close behind him.

'It's Victoria!' shouted Morag, holding Katie up high to give her a better look.

A cheer rose from the crowd.

'That's Cape Otway,' announced the Captain, smiling with relief. 'It's never easy to find this entrance to Bass Strait. When we see that light flashing from the lighthouse there, then we know we're safe. Well done, helmsman!' he called to the man at the wheel. 'And well done, First Mate.'

But just as the people were standing and stretching themselves and getting ready to go below for an hour or two of sleep before breakfast, a chilling cry rang out. It was Janet Matheson. Her white hair had tumbled from her cap. She stood motionless by the open hatchway, gazing back with fixed eyes towards the seaman at the wheel.

'Blood!' she shrieked. 'I see blood! Blood will be spilt on this ship before we come to land!'

Everyone stood frozen with terror.

'Janet does have the Sight!' murmured Effie MacDonald. 'It runs in her family. She's been right before now when she's seen trouble coming.'

'*Whose* blood will be spilt, Janet?' asked Donald firmly, stepping up close to her and looking right into her face. 'Tell us more!'

'I see no more!' she cried. 'All I see is blood!'

Janet's trance suddenly lifted. She blinked her eyes and went meekly below with Alec. Family by family, the people trooped after her in silence. They climbed into their berths and comforted their children. The *Georgiana* ploughed steadily onwards through the rough waters of Bass Strait.

9

Gold Fever!

The pull of the land was too strong to resist. Within a couple of hours they had given up all hope of sleep and had flocked back onto the deck to gaze out at the strange new country. As the ship sailed closer to the shore, they could see dark forests running right down to the water's edge and tall black cliffs where the breakers pounded. They saw long beaches of yellow sand. It was a mysterious place, quite unlike anything they'd ever imagined.

Morag leant out over the rail and sniffed at the salty air.

'What's that lovely smell?' she asked in surprise. 'Something sweet. Like honey. Or like flowers. Whatever is it?'

No one knew. All the people were snuffing the wind now and asking each other what the unfamiliar scent could be. Eight bells rang for the watch to change and Walter MacDougall, his thin shoulders bent forwards, came walking briskly along behind the crowd on his way to take over from the helmsman. His bare feet moved lightly over the deck. Morag thought he might know something about that wonderful scent. He'd been to the Colony before. She pushed through the packed rows till she came face to face with the seaman.

'I can smell something blowing off the land, Mr Mac-Dougall,' she said politely, hoping he'd be pleased to be addressed as 'Mr'. 'Something like flowers. Do you know what it is?'

Walter MacDougall stopped and sniffed the air. He grinned at Morag through his red beard as he recognized the scent on the wind.

'Yes, lassie! That's the smell of springtime all right! Springtime in the Colony with the yellow wattle in blossom and the pink flowers coming out on the gumtrees. Those forests over there are thick with wild flowers! You can just get a whiff of eucalyptus from the gum leaves too. A grand smell, isn't it?'

'But this is October, not springtime!' objected Morag.

'October *is* the springtime here!' said MacDougall, laughing. 'Spring starts in September and it goes on right through October. Then the hot summer starts. You're arriving at just the right time.'

'But what do they do about winter?' she asked him in amazement.

'They have that in June and July. You'll soon get used to it, lassie. Before you've been long in the Colony, you'll think it's perfectly normal to have winter in July and summer at the New Year. But I don't know if you'll ever get used to the blazing heat. Those hot north winds can just about burn the skin off your face. And the dratted flies keep buzzing round your head all day and the mosquitoes come out at night. That's not so good.'

'Do you know anything about the diggings, Mr Mac-Dougall?' she asked him, keeping her voice calm and pleasant. 'That place where people pick up lumps of gold? I think I'd like to go there. With my brother Allan, of course. Not on my own.'

A shadow came over Walter MacDougall's face. He lowered his voice.

'I've never been to the diggings,' he said, 'but I've heard they're rough places. You mustn't think of going there at all, lassie. Not even with your brother. You stick with your family and work with the sheep. That's a much safer life.'

'But wouldn't *you* like to go to the diggings?' she persisted.

He looked cagey and glanced over his shoulder.

'Well, maybe I would and maybe I wouldn't. We'll see about that when we come to Geelong. It's best if you don't ask too many questions about the gold.'

'Hurry along there, MacDougall,' called the First Mate sharply. 'Time you were on the watch. MacNeill's been four hours at that wheel. He wants his breakfast.'

'Aye aye, sir!' said MacDougall, switching into English. 'Sorry, sir. Just got talking with this lassie here.' And he ran aft to relieve MacNeill.

Morag wriggled her way back to her family and explained to anyone who would listen about the smell of the wild flowers in springtime and the odd way the seasons moved in the colony.

'If the summer and the winter are all back to front like that,' she said to her mother, 'then the feet are probably back to front as well! Janet Matheson always said they were.'

'Let's just hope she's not right about the blood,' said Effie, her voice suddenly anxious. 'Twisted feet I can put up with if I have to, but not blood on this ship.'

'There'll be no blood on the ship, Effie love,' said Donald, putting his arm around her. 'Janet's getting old and she has these strange ideas.'

'Father,' said Morag sadly, 'we could be living miles away from Janet when we land in the Colony, couldn't we? Every family'll be sent to a different place. We mightn't ever see her again!'

'I don't think it could be as bad as that, Morag,' said her father. His smile was reassuring. 'It's an island, after all. Surely we could just walk along the glen or over the hill to see our friends again. And we'll probably meet them at the Free Church every Sabbath, just as we did at home.'

Morag wasn't quite convinced. That new country seemed so vast. It looked nothing like Skye. Even the colours were different. The green was a kind of brown.

The *Georgiana* made good progress. Soon she was sailing towards the two Heads that guard the passage into Port Phillip Bay. A flurry of excitement gripped the emigrants. Their bundles of belongings were roped and tied for the last time. But with the excitement came a whiff of fear. The Rip, that stretch of turbulent water between sandy headlands, looked very narrow. Would their ship ever manage to pass between them?

As they came closer to the Heads, the weather turned rough and squally. The ship was forced into a long uncomfortable wait for the pilot while the seamen prowled restlessly about the decks and climbed up into the rigging to watch for him. Even Captain Murray himself seemed as anxious as the crofters and the sailors.

'So near and yet so far!' Morag heard him muttering despondently to the First Mate as he stood gazing out through the rain. The ship bucked and trembled. Her English was better now and she could just follow what he was saying. She guessed at the words she didn't know.

'This waiting's bad, Mr Boyd,' the Captain went on. 'It's bound to get the seamen into a difficult state of mind. We'd better fill up those lifeboats with lumber. That'll stop the men from taking them away when we finally come to port. The Colony's gone mad with gold fever but it's a fever my sailors mustn't catch!'

'I think they might've caught it already, sir,' said the First Mate. 'I hear rumours, you know. There could be trouble brewing.'

'I'll soon put a stop to that!' barked the Captain, sounding sterner than Morag had ever heard him before. 'Get the lumber into those boats at once!'

Mr Boyd gave the orders. Scowling and reluctant, the crew set to work carrying great armfuls of heavy timber and empty wooden boxes up from the hold. They threw them noisily into the boats along the deck. Morag watched, keeping as close as she dared but pretending to read her Shorter Catechism while she sheltered from the wind.

'Everyone's willing to join us except that stubborn lad, Jimmy MacLean,' she heard MacNeill whispering in Gaelic to MacDougall as they paused for a minute. 'He's missing the chance of a lifetime! But at least he won't give us away to the Captain. Jamie Cross made him swear it on the Bible last night. He threatened to punch him again if he didn't swear!'

'We can't trust that boy, Bible or no Bible!' MacDougall mumbled back. 'He could warn the Captain this very night. He might've warned him already. Why's the Captain making us fill up these boats if he hasn't heard something from the boy? We'll have to make him come with us, John. If we leave him here he'll turn informer on every single one of us.'

'We'll talk to him tonight, then,' agreed MacNeill. 'Jimmy'll have to join us or he'll get a knife right in his stomach! Let's show him the knives, John. The knives and the guns. That'll make him see sense. The boy won't argue with the knives!'

'Right!' said MacDougall. 'We'll nobble him tonight.'

Morag stared unseeing at the words of the Catechism. Her eyes were blurred. There was a long pause till the two men were back with their next load of timber.

'But what about these crofters, John?' hissed Mac-Dougall. He sounded scared. 'There are sixty Skye men on this ship! The Captain'd only have to give them a shout and they'd rush at us. We wouldn't stand a chance against the ship's officers and that wild bunch of Highlanders!'

'Just leave them to Jamie Cross!' said MacNeill. 'He's thought about the crofters. He's a clever man, that cook. Thinks of everything. He's going down to have a sharp talk with those men. He'll show *them* the knives! He'll poke a gun in their ribs! He'll tell them straight out that if there's trouble between the crew and the Captain, they're to sit tight and shut up. If they run to his help, they'll lie dead on the deck! Those poor crofters'll be like terrified sheep when Jamie's finished talking to them, Walter. You'll see!'

'Hurry up there, you two!' shouted the First Mate. 'Stop jabbering and bring up another load of lumber.'

'Aye aye, sir!' said MacDougall and MacNeill together.

Morag felt frightened. What should she do? Talk to Jimmy? He was carting timber along with the other seamen. She ran below to find her father. Donald MacDonald was sitting upright at the end of his top berth, his Psalm book in his hands. He was singing under his breath.

'What's the matter, Morag?' he said when he saw her white face.

She clambered up beside him and told him all she'd heard.

'They've got knives, Father, and guns!' she gasped. 'What'll we do? They might kill the Captain if we don't warn him in time!'

'We'll stay right out of it, Morag!' said Donald, his voice sharp with fear. 'Trouble between the Captain and the crew is none of our business.'

Morag was stunned.

'But you've always liked Captain Murray. He's given us a good voyage. Someone ought to warn him. Are you turning against him?'

'I'm not turning against him at all. I'm not taking sides. I'm keeping right out of it. Do you understand?'

Morag nodded glumly.

'Anyway,' added her father, 'more than likely there'll be no trouble. These seamen talk big but they'd never really face the Captain with their knives or their pistols. That'd be mutiny! The whole thing'll blow over.'

Morag wasn't so sure. She'd heard the determination in

the voices of those two sailors. It hadn't seemed like empty talk to her.

By the next morning the wind had dropped and the sea was calm. The pilot's boat appeared at last and a cheer went up from the decks as the pilot himself came on board to guide them in through the Rip. The *Georgiana* sailed easily between the Heads and into a wide sheltered bay. Morag gasped at the beauty of it. Ringed by low hills and green forest, Port Phillip Bay was alive with seabirds. They flew in thick flocks around the ship. They perched in the rigging and floated on the sea. They cried and they called. The air was full of their sound.

The ship skirted a peninsula on their port bow and turned due west into the smaller Corio Bay. And there, straight ahead of them, lay the snug little township of Geelong with blue hills rising behind it. The Captain dropped anchor off Port Henry, well outside the sandbar, and *Georgiana* took her place among sixty other large vessels, all silent and deserted. Their crews had gone off to the diggings. Only the Captains and a handful of officers stood about idly on the empty decks, watching as the new ship came to rest at the end of her long voyage.

Captain Murray called the crofters together under a brilliant sky. The blue waters of Corio Bay sparkled around them in the sunshine. Mr Gilby explained just what was to happen next and Jimmy was on hand to translate. The daily lessons had done some good but English was still a difficult tongue.

The new masters would be coming on board in two days' time – early on Monday morning. Some would be townsfolk looking for servants. Some would be small landowners from the farms and market-gardens close to Geelong. And then there'd be the squatters, the really big landlords from further off in the Western District. They were the sheep men.

'Offer to do anything!' Mr Gilby concluded. 'Refuse to

do nothing! Even your young children can make good workers. And be sure someone in each family is ready to do the talking in English. Most of these squatters come from Scotland but they don't know the Gaelic. Any questions?'

'Yes, sir,' said Donald. 'Little Flora here is the best at English in our family. Do you mean I'd have to let her do the talking to the landlords? That's not right! She's only a child!'

The other crofters grumbled their agreement. The men from Skye were used to doing the talking and making the decisions at home.

'If you men can manage enough English, then you do the talking yourselves,' Mr Gilby said. 'But just check with your little Floras and Kirstys before you agree to anything. It's no use travelling sixty miles from Geelong and then saying you didn't understand.'

'Sixty miles!' everyone gasped.

'Do you mean we might be sixty miles from Geelong, sir?' asked Neil Mackinnon.

'Yes, indeed. You could be a hundred miles from Geelong! Sometimes the best jobs are furthest away. Don't forget to ask what the wages'll be for the whole family. And ask how you're to pay back your loans from the Emigration Society.'

'We don't have to pay them back!' someone objected angrily.

'Yes, we do!' said Donald MacDonald. 'Mr Chant said so.'

Everyone started arguing about whether the money had to be paid back or not.

'Quiet!' roared Mr Gilby, holding up both arms. 'The truth of the matter is that you *do* have to pay it back. A pound or ten shillings a month is the usual way. Your masters will take it out from your wages. Then the money can be used again to bring more folk out here.'

The crowd fell silent.

'Isn't there any way we can stay near our friends?' asked Alec Matheson. 'Talisker folk like to stick together, you see, sir.'

'You might be lucky enough to find a squatter looking for two families,' said Mr Gilby. 'You can always ask. But you mustn't be too fussy. Beggars can't be choosers, you know. At your age, Alec Matheson, you'll be lucky to get any kind of work!'

Tomorrow was the Sabbath, Captain Murray reminded them. Ninety-seven days exactly since they'd sailed from Greenock. There'd be their church service on deck as usual. A day of quietness and rest before they left the ship. He thanked them for the testimonial they'd all signed, with names or just with crosses, in gratitude for a safe journey.

'I'll be taking breakfast in the morning with my friend, the Captain of the *Brilliant* alongside us here,' the Captain ended with a smile. 'But I'll be back on board in good time for the change of watch at noon. Right, you can all go now.'

The families trooped below. Down there, at the far end of the table, Jamie Cross was waiting for them with MacDougall and MacNeill. Their jackets were bulging. The men from Skye huddled around the sailors and muttered anxiously together. Morag couldn't see a thing through the crowd. The men came back to their wives and children, oddly silent and subdued. Jamie Cross was satisfied.

Early the next morning, Allan called Morag up on deck to watch as Jimmy rowed Captain Murray across from the *Georgiana* to the *Brilliant* for breakfast. Everything on board was peaceful in the sunlight. The seamen were going about their usual tasks. The decks were scrubbed clean. Not a sign of trouble anywhere. Morag's fears subsided.

Promptly at twelve o'clock, the Captain arrived back on board, just as he'd promised, and the emigrants went down for their dinner. Just as the meat was being tipped onto the table, an unfamiliar shout rang out from the deck above their heads. It was the voice of Jamie Cross. He was running. His wild cry was followed by the heavy pounding of sailors' feet. All the seamen were shouting now. They were heading for the Captain's cabin. The crofters leapt up from the long table and rushed to the companionway. The women and children followed close behind the men. In a silent crowd they stood at a distance and watched.

With his back to his cabin door, Captain Murray was facing his crew. Mr Gilby stood on his right hand, Mr Boyd and the Second Mate on his left. Jamie Cross glared back at him from the centre of the seventeen seamen, his hair pulled back into a mariner's pigtail, his hands gripping a gun behind his back. The other sailors held long curved knives, pistols, sawn-off shot-guns and thick cudgels. The crofters stared in horror at the weapons. In the midst of the seamen stood Jimmy MacLean. One man grasped him by his left arm and one by his right. He looked around helplessly. His eyes met Morag's and turned away. There was no escape.

'Well, men, what's the matter?' Captain Murray demanded.

It was the cook who answered.

'Captain!' he said, his eyes fierce, his legs well apart. 'We want a boat! We're off to the diggings to make our fortune! Give us a boat or we'll take one by force!'

The sailors behind him roared their assent.

'A boat!' they shouted. 'We're off to the gold! We want a boat!'

Only Jimmy was silent. There were tears in his eyes and he pulled against his captors.

The Captain tried to be reasonable though his face was grim.

'You can't leave the ship, men!' he said. 'That's impossible! We sail for Sydney in a couple of weeks. But I'll make you a promise. When we come back here from Sydney you'll have leave for two months. Then you can go to the diggings. You can all try your luck and still come back to the ship. I can't say fairer than that.'

The sailors grumbled and muttered among themselves.

'We won't go to Sydney!' shouted the Bosun.

'We want a boat now!' bellowed the carpenter.

'Now! Now! Now!' chanted the seamen.

'Right!' called the stout cook, taking charge of the crew. 'Unload that lumber, men!'

The sailors surged forwards to the nearest lifeboat and began pulling the timber out with their strong left hands. In their right hands they still held their weapons. Jimmy was forced to help them with a knife at his throat.

'Come on, you Skye men!' the Captain yelled at the cowed emigrants as he reached back into his cabin for a gun. 'This is a mutiny! I've given you a safe passage! Now *you* must help me!'

'No, sir!' cried Angus MacRae fiercely before anyone else could speak. 'These seamen are armed. They'll blow our brains out if we come to your rescue. They'll cut our throats with their knives. We're not going to stop them!'

Morag moved up close to her father. She pushed him from behind.

'Go on!' she urged. 'Captain Murray's a good man.'

Donald MacDonald hesitated. Then he stepped forward. 'I'll help you, sir!' he cried. His voice shook.

'Oh no, you won't!' snarled Angus MacRae and he pulled him back into the crowd.

'Then I'll help you!' shouted Allan and he leapt across the deck to the Captain's side before anyone could stop him. Morag was astonished. Her brother looked so defence-less.

'I'm coming too!' cried Ewen Gordon and he ran to stand with Allan. No one else moved. The crofters looked shamefaced and embarrassed. They shifted from one foot to the other. They were terrified of the sailors with their guns and their knives.

'Ewen! Come back!' Mistress Gordon called in terror but Ewen stood firm.

The boat was cleared of lumber now. The crew were ready to go. The Captain raised his gun.

'I'll shoot the first man who hooks a tackle to that lifeboat!' he roared.

'Damn your eyes, Captain!' the cook bellowed back at him and he ran to hook the tackle to the boat. He pulled on the fall. With the Bosun and the carpenter to help him and with MacNeill and MacDougall heaving from the other end, he hoisted the boat over the side of the ship.

Captain Murray fired. The cook fell dead on the deck. Blood gushed from the wound in his head.

The crofters gasped. They edged backwards, away from the body, away from the blood. Allan and Ewen rushed forward with the Captain and his officers but they were too few against so many.

At that instant the seamen let fly with their curses and they brandished their weapons. The sailmaker held a gun to the Captain's head. His finger was on the trigger when Allan flung himself bodily at the man and knocked him down. The bullet missed its aim but it grazed the Captain's skull. MacDougall leapt forward and snatched the Captain's own gun from his fingers. He was about to fire at the First Mate when the Surgeon kicked the weapon out of his hand. It clattered to the deck. Blood was flowing from the Captain's head now and he staggered about in pain and confusion, his face white and his eyes full of terror.

MacDougall and MacNeill shoved the Surgeon roughly aside and lashed the Captain to the wheel, pulling his arms and legs out to their fullest extent and tying him so tight he couldn't move. They grabbed Allan next and tied him behind the Captain. They kicked both of them hard in the head and left them for dead. Allan groaned. Meanwhile the rest of the crew chased Ewen and the officers below and fastened down the hatches. The people were stunned into silence.

'Allan!' cried Morag.

'Shut up, girl!' muttered Angus MacRae. 'Let them do their worst! If we speak one word, we'll be as dead as the cook!'

The sailors had their boat in the water. One by one they sprang over the rail and down the ladder. As Morag watched in horror, she saw Jimmy MacLean going over with them, a knife still held at his throat, two seamen still grasping his arms. Jimmy was protesting and crying but the men pushed him and pummelled him into the boat, the knife always pressed to his neck. They pulled on the oars and made for the shore.

The cook lay dead on the deck. The Captain was unconscious and tied to the wheel. Allan's eyes were wide open in pain. He was spread-eagled against the far side of the wheel, his face swollen and bleeding. The officers bellowed from below and hammered in vain on the hatches. Only when the boat had left the ship far behind did the emigrants make a move to let them out. Then the two Mates ran to untie the Captain. He was still alive. Mr Gilby bound up his wounds. Donald released Allan and carried him in his arms to the berths below.

Another boat was cleared of lumber and lowered over the side. The officers lifted the groaning Captain to the boat and rowed him ashore to find urgent help for his injuries. They'd report the mutiny and soon the troopers would be riding off after the sailors on their way to the diggings. The crofters retreated below and crouched shivering on their bunks. The body of Jamie Cross lay on the deck in the heat of the day.

'Blood!' murmured Janet Matheson from under her blanket. 'I said there'd be blood!'

Morag helped her mother to wash Allan's face. He had

bruises and cuts on his head and one of his teeth was missing. He flinched with the pain. His body trembled with shock. Then Morag heaved herself onto her own berth and held Katie tight in her arms. She thought about Jimmy, forced into the boat by those men. What would they do to him now? Slowly she fell into a troubled sleep, broken by terrible dreams.

10

Mr Reekie

When Morag woke again, late on that Sunday afternoon, her father was already stirring in the bunk above. He'd been sleeping too, like everyone else. Sleep was about the only escape from the violence they'd seen.

'We'd better do something about that body,' Donald was muttering to Alec Matheson. 'It's not right to leave it lying there on the deck. The man may have been a mutineer but there's a respect we show to the dead.'

'What can we do?' asked Alec, propping himself up on one elbow.

'We could cover the body, at least. And we could move it into the shade.'

'We shouldn't move it, Donald!' said Alec quickly. 'There's sure to be an inquest about that death. Was it a lawful killing or was it murder? The police'll be coming out from Geelong. They'll want to see the body lying exactly where it fell.'

'You can't call it murder!' put in Neil MacKinnon. 'Jamie Cross was defying the Captain! It was mutiny! The Captain was right to shoot!'

'Thou shalt not kill!' said Donald MacDonald. 'That's what the Good Book says!'

Morag suddenly spoke up from her berth below.

'But Father, if you and the other men had only gone to the Captain's help, he wouldn't have had to shoot! We're all to blame! We all killed the cook! All except Allan and Ewen!'

'Don't be silly, Morag,' said her mother sharply from the far end of the berth.

'You're right, Donald,' said Alec. 'We should cover the body, at least. Come on, we'll do it now. We'll find an old sail and spread it over the poor man.'

Donald followed Alec up the companionway. That was the signal for everyone else to climb out of the berths and to start talking to each other again in nervous voices. Shock and fear still gripped them.

'What'll we eat?' asked Kenny, starting to cry. 'The cook's dead! Who'll cook the food? I'm hungry!'

'I can hear a boat coming, Kenny!' said Morag, wanting to distract him. 'Listen! There are the oars. Let's go up and see what's happening.'

Before the mothers had a chance to hold them back, most of the children made a dash for the stairs. They blinked as they rushed into the blazing sunlight. A boat had just reached the ship and behind it came another. Mr Gilby climbed on board with the Mates. Three policemen in big hats followed them up. They strode towards the body.

By the time the sergeants had taken statements from the emigrants and the officers and had called on six men to lower the cook's heavy body to the police boat, the sun had set.

The MacDonalds stood with the other families along the rail to watch the police boat moving slowly away, past the line of deserted ships and towards the shadowy land. They listened to the fading splash of the oars.

'What a terrible start to our new life in Victoria!' said Effie.

'I'm still hungry!' bawled Kenny.

Everyone was hungry now. Donald spoke to Mr Gilby and came back with the news that there'd be nothing to eat tonight except dry oatmeal with fresh water poured over it. Tomorrow the mess-groups would have to appoint a couple of cooks to boil up the beef and potatoes and to make the porridge and brew the tea.

'That's women's work!' sneered Angus MacRae. 'The men can't do it!'

'But the women aren't allowed in the galley,' said Effie. 'It's a rule of the ship.'

'That's only when the crew's on board,' said Donald. 'All the sailors have gone now so I think you women can go into the galley.'

'Well, I'm not cooking tonight!' declared Effie. 'Let's just get out our oatmeal. It won't be the first time we've eaten uncooked oats with water.'

Kenny was delighted to have food at last. He mixed the oats and water into a sticky mush with his fingers and began to eat. Luckily the Matron was nowhere to be seen. Ever since the moment when the cook had been killed, she had shut herself away in her cabin with the door locked behind her.

'Allan,' said Morag, coming close to the berth. 'Can you eat something?'

Allan opened his eyes and moved his head carefully.

'Not hungry,' he murmured.

Morag bent down to him.

'You were brave, Allan!' she said quietly so no one else could hear. 'I was so proud of you!'

Allan smiled up at her through his cracked lips. The gap in his teeth was red and sore. He settled himself to sleep again.

'Four men needed to scrub the deck!' bellowed the Second Mate, coming down to look for volunteers.

'Not the whole deck!' protested Neil MacKinnon. 'We'd be scrubbing all night.'

'No, no, not the whole deck. Just the patch of blood. Come on! Who'll lend a hand?'

No one was very keen on the idea but at last Neil

MacKinnon and Donald MacDonald stepped forward with two men from Portree.

As Morag lay down on her bunk again she could hear four brushes scrubbing and scrubbing at the blood on the deck.

Early on Monday morning everyone was up early to watch out for the arrival of the farmers. Even Allan went with them, his head swathed in a white bandage, his arms still painful and stiff.

'They're coming!' cried Flora. 'Look!'

A line of small black boats was moving out towards the *Georgiana*. Soon the orderly line turned into a race, the rowers pulling hard on the oars, each boat trying to get there first.

'They must be desperate for workers,' said Morag.

'Most of their shepherds and servants have probably run off to dig for gold,' said her father. 'We've come at a good time.'

As the newcomers hurried on board, the emigrants stared at them anxiously, wondering just which man might prove a good master and which one a tyrant. It was hard to tell from their faces. These Colonial men looked much alike, their faces gnarled and brown from years under the sun. They all wore high black boots, moleskin trousers of strong cotton twill, red or blue shirts and wide-brimmed hats. Each man found a place on the deck, sat himself down on a box and looked around at the families from Skye.

'Come on now, you good Island folk!' one of them called out in a loud, friendly voice. 'Who wants a place as a shepherd near Colac? Seventy pounds a year for the right man and full rations! Free slops as well.'

'Slops?' said Morag more loudly than she'd meant to.

'That means clothes, lassie. And the lucky man'll get free food and a hut to live in. Pity your father's got such a big family! I'm only looking for single men. Families have too

many mouths to feed. Come on now! Who's for Colac?
Only fifty miles to the west!'

Two young men from the south of Skye stepped forward
and within a few minutes the deal was done. They shook
hands on it.

'Get your baggage straight away, lads, and we'll be off,'
said their new master.

'You're crazy to take on single men, Joe!' called one of
the other farmers cheerfully. He was a big man with a wild
bushy beard. His red shirt was checked with blue. 'Single
men run off to the diggings! Family men stay put. I'm
looking for a family man myself. Two or three family men
in fact. We've just lost four more of our shepherds at *Brolga
Marsh*. All I've got left now's the convicts and the
blacks!'

'Let's try that man, Donald,' urged Effie. 'He says he
wants a family.'

Donald took a few steps across the deck, his family close
beside him.

'Come on now,' said the big man from *Brolga Marsh*.
'What's your name and what can you do?'

'Donald MacDonald from Talisker on Skye,' said
Donald, speaking deliberately. 'I was shepherd to MacLeod
of MacLeod. I have a wife and four – I mean five children.'
He paused. 'Are you what they call the swatter?' he asked,
struggling to pronouce the strange word.

'Squatter!' repeated Flora more clearly. 'Are you the
squatter, sir?'

The big man smiled at her.

'No, lassie, I'm no squatter, worst luck! I'm Bob Reekie,
the overseer of *Brolga Marsh*. Mr William Martin's the
squatter. Fine English gentleman, he is too. And *Brolga
Marsh* is the best sheep and cattle run west of Ballarat!
Mr Martin owns it but I'm the one that runs it! Poor
Mr Martin hardly knows one end of a sheep from the
other but he's a good man all the same. Always reading

books. That's his only trouble!' He laughed a big hearty laugh that shook his enormous chest under the checked shirt.

'An Englishman?' said Donald MacDonald, his voice suddenly suspicious.

'Don't let that worry you, Donald,' said Bob Reekie quickly. 'He's a good man although he's English. And I'm a true Scot myself. Born on a farm near Aberdeen!'

Donald looked a great deal happier when he caught the word 'Aberdeen'.

'What wages are you offering, sir?' he asked. 'My English is not so good but little Flora here can help me.'

'Wages? First I'll need to know what your family can do, Donald. Let's start with your good wife there.'

Flora rushed in before her father had a chance.

'My mother can milk cows, sir, and make butter. And she can cook.'

'Good. Your mother can be the hut-keeper and she'll help my wife with the dairy and the cooking. Now what about your big sister?'

Morag did not want Flora speaking for her.

'I'm used to milking, sir,' she said quickly. 'And I'd like to learn to be a housemaid too.'

Mr Reekie beamed down at her.

'You can learn to be a housemaid all right,' he said. 'My wife'll teach you herself! Mrs Reekie's the housekeeper to Mr Martin. Best housekeeper west of Ballarat! Now little Flora, what about you?'

'I could be a nursemaid! Does Mr Martin have lots of children, sir?'

'No children at all,' said Mr Reekie. 'No wife either. Mr Martin's a bachelor. But Mrs Reekie and I could do with a nursemaid. We've got a bonny wee baby only three years old and no one to look after him since the last silly girl ran off with a shearer to fossick for gold.'

Flora nodded, highly pleased with herself.

Mr Reekie pushed back his hat and turned to look at Allan.

'What's the matter with your face, lad? Been fighting?'

Allan mumbled something and Flora explained.

'You sound like a good lad to me!' said the overseer. 'How old are you?'

'Nearly fifteen, sir,' said Allan.

'And do you speak good English like this little Flora here?'

'I'm up to Question 84, sir,' said Allan through his sore mouth. 'In the Shorter Catechism. Angus MacRae was teaching us on the ship.'

'Well, come on lad, tell me then. What is Question 84 and what's the answer? I had to learn it myself once, when I was a lad in Aberdeenshire.'

Allan took a deep breath and looked desperately round at his father and mother. Then he spoke slowly, his voice chanting the words all on one sad monotonous note, just as Angus MacRae had taught him to do it.

'"What doth every sin deserve? Every sin deserveth God's wrath and curse, both in this life, and that which is to come."'

'Well, well, well!' said Mr Reekie, one hand across his mouth to hide a smile. 'And what about sheep and cattle and horses? Did this Angus MacRae give you handy words like dipping and shearing, mustering and branding, scab and foot-rot?'

'No, sir,' said Allan, quite bewildered. 'He just taught us about sin.'

'Never mind, boy. I'll soon tell you the words you need. I like a lad with courage. And that wee brother of yours can be a watchman to keep off the howling dingoes at night!'

Kenny glanced nervously at his father.

'Don't worry, Kenny!' said Donald in fast Gaelic. 'Who

cares about a few old dingoes, whatever they are? Just ask him again about the pay, Flora. That's all we need to know.'

'How much money will we get, sir?' asked Flora.

'For the whole family, one hundred and twelve pounds a year and the usual rations and slops. And a good hut to live in. Nice bark roof, neat split-log walls. Best hut west of Ballarat.'

'But what about a little croft, sir?' asked Donald. 'For growing our potatoes and a few rows of oats. And will you let us keep a cow for the milk?'

'You crofters are all the same! Always wanting a bit of land for your potatoes!' Mr Reekie smiled. 'Yes, there's a goodish piece of wild scrub all around the hut. You can have that rent-free, Donald, if you'll clear it yourselves. You won't have much time to work it, mind. Only the evenings. You'll be busy with the sheep all day long. And I'll sell you a cow for two shillings a month. You'll soon feel at home at *Brolga Marsh*.'

'What's a brolga, sir?' asked Morag.

'Brolgas? They're birds. Big birds like cranes. They dance! Like this!' and Bob Reekie jumped off his stool and began to leap about the deck on his long legs, his arms waving up and down like wings, his head bowing low and then stretching up high. Everyone burst into laughter.

'We'll come!' said Donald MacDonald, holding out his hand to Mr Reekie. Morag was excited. One hundred and twelve pounds a year! And food and a hut and a croft of their own! Never in all their lives had they had such wealth!

'Right,' said Mr Reekie briskly. 'Now I need two more families. One more for our own out-station and one for our neighbour, Mr Adams, up the track at *Pittencairn*.'

'There's Mistress Gordon and her boys and Kirsty,' suggested Morag.

'Bring them here!' cried Mr Reekie. 'I'd like a family with boys. Just what I need. Flora dashed off to find Mistress Gordon.

'And one more family?' he asked.

'There's the Mathesons,' said Morag uncertainly, 'though Alec's fairly old. But his son Tomas is a strong man.'

'Let me see them!'

As Kenny went off to hunt for the Mathesons, Flora ran up leading Mistress Gordon by one hand. Ewen, Calum and Kirsty came close behind.

'This is our friend, Mistress Gordon, sir,' said Flora. 'She speaks good English. She can cook too.'

'And where's your man?' asked Mr Reekie, smiling at Mistress Gordon.

'He's dead, sir. Died in the famine. But my two boys work as well as any man. Ewen's fifteen.'

'Sorry. You'll need a husband if you're going to live out in the bush. A woman on her own has a terrible time in this Colony. It's not safe. I think you'd do better to find a quiet place here in Geelong.'

'I can look after myself!' said Mistress Gordon sharply.

'You must have a man,' said Mr Reekie, 'or I can't take you.'

'I know a man!' cried Morag and she hurried off to find Alasdair Nicolson and his two little girls. They were wandering hopelessly from one farmer to the next. No one wanted a man who had two children but no wife. There were tears in his eyes.

'They won't take the girls!' he said indignantly to Morag. 'They told me to put them into an orphanage! What would my poor Anna say?'

'Come on,' urged Morag. 'Mr Reekie just might take you. He needs an extra man.'

She told Mr Reekie how Anna Nicolson had been blown off the ship and how Alasdair Nicolson had to look after his two girls.

'He doesn't want to put them in an orphanage,' she said.

'That's perfect!' cried Mr Reekie, rubbing his hands and

looking from Mistress Gordon to Alasdair Nicolson. 'Here we've got a fine tall woman without a husband and a splendid young man without a wife. Now if you two will just agree to get married tomorrow, you can come as one family to *Brolga Marsh*.'

'Married!' gasped Mistress Gordon.

Alasdair Nicolson's face went white.

'But I'm a few years older than Alasdair Nicolson,' objected Mistress Gordon. 'And we hardly know each other. And his poor wife's only been dead a few weeks. He couldn't think of marrying again so soon.'

'If you agree to marry, you can come to *Brolga Marsh* tomorrow,' said Mr Reekie firmly. 'If you won't marry, I can't take you. There's only one spare hut waiting up there at the out-station. If you're going to live in one hut together, you'll have to be married. Mr Martin wouldn't think of anything else.'

'Please, Mother,' whispered Kirsty. 'Do marry Alasdair Nicolson. Then I can go on helping with his children. They're so good.'

'Please, Father,' said the two little Nicolson girls, pulling on his hands. 'Do marry Mistress Gordon. She's always kind to us and we love her big Kirsty.'

Mistress Gordon and Alasdair Nicolson stared at each other for a long minute.

'You're a good woman,' he said to her at last. 'I'm willing enough – if you'll have me.'

Mistress Gordon nodded.

'I'm willing,' she said. 'You don't have to love me, Alasdair Nicolson. It'll just be an arrangement. An arrangement to get us this place and a roof over our heads. You're an honest man and I like you. I liked your wife, Anna, too. Is that enough?'

'It's enough, Mistress Gordon,' said Alasdair Nicolson. 'With God's help, the loving will come later.'

'You must call me Shona, now, not Mistress Gordon,'

she said quietly and then she turned back to Mr Reekie and spoke in English.

'We're willing to marry,' she said.

'Good! That's what I like to hear. We'll find that Free Church minister in Geelong tomorrow. It'll only take a minute. Now where are those Mathesons you were telling me about?'

Kenny appeared at that very moment with the Mathesons. Alec had the fiddle under his arm. Janet's white hair was neatly coiled under a clean cap. Their son, Tomas, came with Rachel his wife, the boy Murdo and the toddling baby.

'Hmm!' said Mr Reekie doubtfully as he looked at Alec and Janet. 'You seem a bit old to be of much use to Mr Adams. What can you do?'

'Alec can play the fiddle, sir,' said Morag, 'and he knows all the old songs and dances. And Janet's the story-teller and she has the Second Sight.'

Mr Reekie laughed loudly but not unkindly.

'But Alec's a good shepherd too, sir,' Morag added quickly, 'and so's Tomas. Please take them! They're our friends!'

'They'll do!' said Mr Reekie. 'One hundred and twelve pounds a year for the whole family. Pay off your debt to the Society at ten shillings a month. All right? Sign here then, Alec Matheson.'

Alec made his cross on the paper.

'How far will we be from the Mathesons, Mr Reekie?' asked Morag.

'Not far, lassie. They'll be at the very next sheep-run. *Pittencairn*'s only twelve miles from *Brolga Marsh*.'

'Twelve miles!' said Morag.

'Twelve miles are nothing in the bush!'

Mr Reekie was stuffing his papers back into his pocket and getting ready to leave the ship. His cheerful smile had faded.

'Now there's something I want to say to you all,' he said sternly, looking around at his three families. 'You people from the Highlands don't have a very good reputation in this Colony. Everyone knows you're honest, of course, but everyone says you're lazy and dirty! I expect hard work from every one of you. I don't ever want to see you men sitting about watching the women do all the work or waiting for the rain to stop! Is that understood?'

Everyone nodded. The women and girls smiled to themselves.

'And there'll be creek water to wash in. We expect you to use it. All right?'

Everyone nodded again.

'Good! That's settled then. I'll be sending a couple of boats out for you at eight in the morning. Be sure you're ready with your baggage. I'll be waiting by Mack's Hotel. We'll just pause at the minister's house for the wedding. It won't take a minute. Till tomorrow then. At Mack's Hotel!'

And with a wave of his hand, Mr Reekie climbed down over the side to his waiting boat. The three families stood in silence and watched him go.

Morag searched up and down the ship for Rory MacRae and came across him sitting alone on a coil of rope near the foot of the main mast.

'We're leaving in the morning,' she told him. 'We've found a good place with work for us all. Out in the bush.'

Rory made no reply.

'Will you be going tomorrow too?' she asked.

He shook his head.

'Not yet. We're staying on board for another two weeks. Mr Boyd's given my father some more carpentry work to do. Then we'll be taking a ship across the water to Van Diemen's Land. That's where the convicts live.'

'But how will you find your mother?' asked Morag.

'I don't know. She's somewhere in a place called Hobart Town. My father says we're sure to find her.'

'Will she be pleased to see him again?' persisted Morag.

'I don't think so,' said Rory, his voice quiet and hard.

There was silence for a minute or two.

'How could I find you?' asked Rory suddenly, looking embarrassed and staring out at the bay. 'If I ever get away from my father.'

'We'll be on a sheep-run called *Brolga Marsh*,' said Morag. 'It's owned by Mr William Martin. West of Ballarat. I do hope we see you again one day, Rory.'

'I hope so too!' said Rory, looking up at her quickly with his dark eyes. 'I'll get there somehow. But I must find my mother first, Morag. It was all my fault, you see. I stole the sheep but she got the blame. I just want to tell her I'm sorry.'

And without another word, Rory jumped off his coil of rope and ran away along the deck.

That night Morag wrote home to the minister at Carbost.

Dear Mr Cameron,

We've arrived safely in the Colony at last but there was a mutiny and the cook was killed by the Captain and Allan was tied to the wheel. But we've found a good place to work on Mr William Martin's sheep-run at Brolga Marsh.

The voyage was terribly long and I got tired of the cramped space and the peculiar smells on the ship and even the salted meat. Now we're feeling nervous about the journey into the bush. We'll be travelling on a bullock dray for ninety miles or more. Mr Reekie told us about some wild animals. I hope we don't meet them.

The new country looks very strange from here. The trees are a different green and the sky's always blue. We can smell the scent of the flowers and there are birds all around the ship. Flora drives me mad with her perfect English and Allan's been so friendly with Ewen Gordon that I haven't seen him as often as I used to do at home but since he had his head kicked he seems much nicer to me. I've made some good friends too. There's Kirsty Gordon and there's Rory MacRae and there's poor Jimmy MacLean, the ship's-

*boy, but the sailors took him away with them so I don't suppose
I'll ever see him again.*

*My mother and father send you their respectful good wishes,
Morag MacDonald.*

The three families were awake early. The last goodbyes
were said to their old friends from Talisker and to the new
friends they'd made on the ship.

'Party for Bob Reekie from *Brolga Marsh*?' shouted a
voice from a boat as it reached the ship. Another boat came
close behind it.

'Here we are!' called Flora over the rail, full of confidence and eager to be the one to talk.

'Hurry up, then!' called the boatmen. 'Send down your
bundles first!'

One by one the bundles and boxes were lowered to the
waiting boats. Then Donald sent down his foot-plough.
The boatmen laughed when they saw it. Cautiously Alec
Matheson put first one leg and then the other over the rail.
He climbed down the rope ladder. Janet came next and then
the rest of the Matheson family. Then Mistress Gordon and
Alasdair Nicolson and all the five children. Then came
Allan and Morag, Flora and Kenny, and then little Katie in
Effie's arms. Last of all came Donald MacDonald himself,
the shepherd from Talisker.

As the two boats pulled away towards Geelong, Morag
looked back at the *Georgiana*. The ship shone in the sunlight
and dipped gently in the water. Under her bowsprit the
white-faced figure of the woman still smiled her patient
wooden smile. Morag caught sight of Rory MacRae, high
on the quarter deck, watching them go. He waved one
long thin arm in farewell and Morag waved back. She had
tears in her eyes. But when she could see him no longer,
she turned towards the township and felt a sudden surge
of excitement. Geelong! Their new life in the Colony was
about to begin!

11

Up Country

By Mack's Hotel Mr Reekie was waiting on his high brown horse. A white sheepdog frisked around the horse's heels. Eight enormous horned bullocks, yoked in pairs, were sprawled on the ground, patiently chewing their cud, and behind them stood the heavily-laden dray, packed with stores for the next six months. On the hotel step lounged another man, short and squat. His hat was even broader in the brim than Mr Reekie's, the skin of his face was browner and more wrinkled, his grey beard was wilder and hung to his waist. A long whip stood propped behind him against the wall. The man tipped back his head and drank thirstily from a rusty tin can. He shouted for more through the open doorway and the landlord came out to fill his can again. The October day was warm already. The sky, as blue as the sea, was immense.

'He needs our scissors!' said Kenny, staring fascinated at the hairy man on the step.

'Shh!' said his mother though her eyes, too, were fixed on the extraordinary beard.

'Right, O'Hara!' Mr Reekie called down to him from his horse. 'Not another drop of that grog! Here come our three Highland families, all ready to go up country. I'll have them on the dray in half a minute. Pick up that whip of yours and get your beasts onto their legs!'

O'Hara didn't move. He was clearly determined to finish

his drink. Mr Reekie turned his attention to the crofters. He slid down from his horse and took charge. The dog sprang forwards as if to welcome the people from Skye and even leaped up against Donald MacDonald's chest, tugging playfully at his brown plaid, licking at his hand. He seemed to know a shepherd when he saw one.

'Down, Sandy, down!' shouted Mr Reekie and the dog came to heel.

'Right, bags and boxes on first!' said Mr Reekie. 'We'll pack them here along the back. All those shepherds' crooks of yours can be stowed in between the sacks. Good heavens! What on earth's that thing, man?'

He'd just caught sight of Donald MacDonald's heavy foot-plough, the beloved *cas chrom* that had been carried safely across the world in the ship's hold.

'It's for digging our croft!' said Donald, holding it tight.

'Is that what they use on Skye?' asked Mr Reekie, still incredulous.

Donald nodded. Mr Reekie didn't laugh.

'Things are very different here,' he said. 'Still, it could come in handy. Just put it along the side there and all of you climb on board. You can sit anywhere around the edge or up on top of the sacks of flour and sugar or on those chests of tea if you like. But mind you don't tumble off. It's a long way to the ground.'

'How fast do you go?' asked Donald, looking at the passive bullocks.

'Not fast,' said Mr Reekie. 'Slow, in fact.'

'Then I think I'll walk. It's good to feel the land under our feet again. Allan and Morag, you can walk with me.'

The women and the younger children climbed onto the dray and found a comfortable spot where their legs could dangle over the edge or a sack where they could perch.

'Come on, O'Hara!' shouted Mr Reekie, mounting his horse again. 'You're the worst bullocky west of Ballarat!'

The man on the step began to move. He stood up and

spat noisily into the dust. He poked his tin can into a gap between the sacks at the back of the dray where Morag caught a glimpse of a large green bottle, and he took up his whip. With a chilling cry and a string of curses, the bullocky whirled the long whip above his head and let it crack high in the air like the terrible blast from a gun. All the children on the dray began to cry.

'Git up there, you dratted critters!' bellowed O'Hara and slashed his whip along the line of crouching bullocks. They staggered to their feet, turned their frightened eyes this way and that, tossed their sharp horns, bent their shoulders to the yokes and began to pull.

'First stop, Yarra Street!' cried Mr Reekie. 'And we'll have that wedding! I'll ride on ahead and tell the minister we're coming!'

He prodded his horse and trotted smartly along the wide dusty street towards the town, the white dog running close behind.

Morag looked up at Mistress Gordon sitting stiffly beside Alasdair Nicolson at the back of the dray. Her face was still. Alasdair had an arm around each of his children and he stared up at the vast sky as if he couldn't quite believe it was real.

Morag found it strange to be walking on solid ground again. She felt giddy after those three months tipping about on a ship at sea. The earth seemed to heave under her feet. Allan, his face still swathed in bandages, must have been feeling much the same. She saw him put out one hand to hold onto the edge of the dray. He slid his other hand inside his shirt and brought out something wooden and brown.

'Look Morag!' he said. 'Neil MacKinnon gave it to me.'

'What is it?'

'It's a chanter for the bagpipes. Neil's got two of them so he gave this one to me. He says I can learn to play on

132

the chanter and one day I might get hold of a full set of pipes. Then I'd be a real piper!'

Morag took the chanter and turned it over in her hands. The wood was smooth, the holes neat and round.

'It's lovely!' she said, torn between admiration and envy. 'You'll be a fine piper, Allan.'

Allan smiled his gappy, crooked smile.

The wide streets of Geelong were straight and dusty. The bullocks plodded slowly up Swanston Street and then, with much shouting from O'Hara and much cracking of his whip, swung right into Ryrie Street. Morag and Allan stared around at the fine houses, the shops and warehouses, the noisy taverns, the rough crowds of people bustling about, the laden wagons and carts, the horses, the long strings of bullocks, the endless hubbub.

'Look at their feet!' cried Morag in delight, her eyes fixed on the perfectly normal feet of all the jostling people in the street. 'They're not back to front at all!'

'Dirty Highlanders!' roared a coarse drunken voice from a window over their heads. 'Go back where you came from! We don't want you here with your filthy plaids and your ugly bonnets! You're lazier than the Irish and that's saying something!'

Morag turned her head away.

'And you can't even speak decent English!' the voice raged on. 'Foreigners! That's what you are! Highland scum. Go back where you came from and eat your rotten potatoes! We don't want you here!'

Fear gripped the crofters. They had never expected a reception like this. The rude voice from the window made Morag feel like an intruder in a hostile world.

The bullocks turned into Yarra Street and stopped outside a terrace of two-storey houses. Mr Reekie stood waiting in a doorway with the minister.

'Let the bride and groom come in and a couple of witnesses!' he called. 'That's all we need.'

Mistress Gordon and Alasdair Nicolson stepped down from the dray and walked slowly to the door. Donald MacDonald and Alec Matheson followed close behind.

While she waited in the street with Allan and Ewen, Morag watched a gang of men loading an odd assortment of goods and chattels onto their cart. There were fat rolls of blue blankets, coils of rope, picks and shovels, a sack of flour, a bag of tobacco, half a dozen buckets, billy-cans with wire handles, flat tin dishes, a black frying pan and a wooden contraption like a cradle. A tired old horse stood between the shafts.

'We're off to the diggin's!' one of the men shouted excitedly to Allan as he heaved up his last shovel with a crash. 'You look a strong lad, sonny, though someone's been bashing you. Want to join us?'

Allan shook his head.

'We'll soon be rich!' laughed another. 'Forest Creek! Buninyong! Mount Alexander! We don't care where we go, so long as we get the gold!'

'Right! We're ready! All aboard!' shouted a third.

Four of the men leaped onto the cart. Another took hold of the reins and led the horse from the front. The sixth man walked behind. He started up a cheerful song and the others joined in. A few of the bystanders waved them off.

'Good luck, you diggers!' someone shouted.

The newly-married couple were just coming out of the minister's house. Mistress Gordon – or Mistress Nicolson as she now was – was red with embarrassment as she held onto Alasdair Nicolson's awkward arm. The two little Nicolson girls hopped down from the dray and ran to hug their father.

'We've got a new mother!' one of them shouted in excitement. Her father looked down at her in surprise at this sudden burst of happiness. Could she have forgotten his dearest Anna so soon?

Alec Matheson limped out past the bride and groom and stood with his back to the dray. He drew the bow across the strings of his fiddle and launched into a merry jig. Janet slid down from the sacks and began to dance around the dray, her bare feet kicking the black earth from the roadway, her skirts held up in her hands, her hair tumbling to her shoulders. The bridal couple smiled sheepishly.

'Hurry along now!' called Mr Reekie. 'No time for dancing! We've got to get on our way. Up you go there, Shona Nicolson!'

The whip cracked and the bullocks began to move. The dray rolled forward in a thick cloud of dust. At the edge of the town, O'Hara took the road to the north-west, past a roughly painted arrow labelled 'Gold'. On each side of the track stood grey-green trees. Morag looked at their strangely knotted branches and their narrow hanging leaves. The road began to climb.

'Are we really going to the diggings?' she called up excitedly to Mr Reekie on his horse.

'No, lassie, we're not. But we're starting off on the track to the diggings right enough, and you'll see plenty of diggers coming and going. But then we'll turn off this diggings road just before O'Meara's inn and we'll make for Linton Park.'

'Will it take us long to get to *Brolga Marsh*?'

'Not long. Only a week if the going's good.'

Morag gasped. A whole week on this track! They'd end up so far from the sea!

'It could be ten days or more if it rains,' said Mr Reekie cheerfully.

'Is this the bush?' asked Allan, gazing at the strange trees. Some of them had been burnt black but already they were sprouting fresh shoots of green.

'No, I wouldn't call this the bush, though it was all wild bush twenty years back before the settlers came. We had a bad fire through here last year. Wait till we cross the river. Then you'll see the real bush. That's the forest country and the wide-plain country.'

They trudged along the rutted track, listening to the creaking wheels of the dray and the ear-splitting yells of O'Hara and the fearsome crack of his whip across the backs of his patient beasts. Morag suddenly felt a wave of sadness sweeping over her. She kept thinking of all those other Skye families from the ship, now scattering to the four corners of this Colony, plodding away into the bush beside dozens of different bullock-drays. They'd all lived so close on the *Georgiana* but she knew they'd probably never see each other again.

Carts crammed with eager young men rattled past the crofters and hurtled on towards the diggings. Ahead and behind were other slow-moving bullock-drays, each enveloped in a great cloud of dust. Most diggers were walking, a swag of blankets across their backs. Morag scanned every face that hurried past, hoping to see Jimmy and the sailors but there was no sign of them. She turned her eyes to the grimy miners who were on their way back from the diggings, bellowing out their good fortune to anyone who would listen or slinking along in glum disappointment. Morag seldom saw a woman on the road. It was a man's world. As she waved her hands around her head to drive off the maddening flies, she suddenly caught sight of a family of black people standing half-naked in the shade of the trees and gazing in bewilderment at the endless stream of noisy diggers. Morag stared in astonishment.

At Batesford on the Moorabool River, the bullock-dray came to a halt.

'We'll take a rest before we cross,' said Mr Reekie.

Allan and Ewen ran to help O'Hara as he unyoked his beasts and led them to the water to drink. Mr Reekie had tethered his horse and was lighting a fire with dry twigs.

He filled a large black can from the river and set it in the middle of the flames.

'We'll just boil up the billy,' he said. 'There's a leg of cold mutton to eat and two fresh loaves of bread from Geelong. Come on now, Donald MacDonald! Call all your good folk under this tree. We're ready to eat!'

Mr Reekie threw two handfuls of tea into the boiling billy of water and stirred the brew with a stem of green gum leaves.

'That just makes it taste better,' he said to Morag. 'You bring all the pannikins for me, lassie. They're in that brown box on the dray.'

Morag found the box and staggered across to the shade where Mr Reekie was carving the mutton into thick slices. Morag handed out the tin pannikins and Mr Reekie filled each one with steaming tea.

'Eat up, man!' he said sharply to Donald who was looking in amazement at the great pile of mutton.

'Will I ask the blessing, sir, or will you?' Donald said hesitantly.

'A blessing?' laughed Mr Reekie. 'For a meal on the track? We don't usually bother. But go ahead, man, if it makes you feel better.'

The three families gathered close around Donald. He pulled off his cap and launched into a long Gaelic prayer of thanksgiving to God for the safe landfall and for this good food in front of them. Mr Reekie stood very still, the billy of tea in his hand, his eyes shut tight. Now and then, as Donald paused in his flow, Mr Reekie opened his eyes for an instant, thinking that perhaps the prayer had come to an end. When the 'Amen' was reached at last, O'Hara had joined them, bringing his green bottle and his old tin can.

'I'm thinkin' that's somethink very like the Irish you've been speakin' there!' he said to Donald in surprise as he filled his can from the bottle and took a swig. 'I could understand you. Or almost. I never knew you poor High-landers could speak the Irish!'

'It's not the Irish at all!' said Donald stiffly. 'It's our own language. The Gaelic. We come from a different country altogether.'

'Sounds much the same to me,' said O'Hara. ''Ere! 'Ave some grog, mate!' And he poured a generous measure from his green bottle right into Donald's pannikin of tea. Donald frowned at the brimming liquid.

'Drink it up, man!' muttered Mr Reekie right in his ear. 'Never offend a bullocky! If he says it's Irish you're speaking, just agree with him or we'll never get this dray home to *Brolga Marsh*.'

Donald meekly sipped the tea and grog and smiled nervously at O'Hara.

'Irish!' he murmured politely. 'Irish and Gaelic! You're quite right, Mr O'Hara! They're much the same really.'

O'Hara grinned back at him, showing the wide black gaps between his teeth. He raised his tin can in a salute of friendship.

'No need for no "Mr", mate. Jist call me Danny. Danny O'Hara from County Clare. Best bullocky west of Ballarat!' he added with a wink.

When the meal was over, Danny O'Hara stretched out on his back and fell asleep. Mr Reekie did the same. First Kenny and Flora, then the older children and finally all the weary grown-ups put their heads down on the ground, where fallen gum-nuts and long grass scratched their cheeks. Everyone slept through the noonday heat and woke to cross the river.

Mr Reekie didn't trust the new bridge to bear the weight of his heavy bullocks. He preferred the ford. He rode on ahead through the shallow water, his white dog swimming beside him. Danny O'Hara plunged in next, swinging his whip in circles over his head, poking and swearing at the front bullocks till they stepped into the current. Soon all eight beasts were splashing their way across the ford and the dray was rolling along silently behind them with the Highlanders perched high on the bulging sacks. Morag stared down in horrified fascination at the swirling water although it never rose more than halfway up the wheels of the dray. Alec Matheson gripped his fiddle to the top of his white head. As the bullocks pulled the dripping dray up the slope on the far side of the Moorabool, a smiling relief broke out on all the Highland faces. The danger was past.

'Six more creeks still to come!' shouted Mr Reekie, amused at their terror.

Now they were really in the bush. A scattered forest of magnificent eucalyptus trees reared up from the plains on each side of the track. Mr Reekie named them in turn. Ribbony gums and swamp gums, messmates and peppermints. Between the dull green of the gumtrees, with their immense trunks and high crowns, Morag saw the delicate wattle trees in blue-green feathery leaves and ablaze with yellow blossom. In the long brown grass grew strange wild flowers – startlingly blue, pink, purple, white. She'd never expected this new country to be so beautiful! It was not the soft misty beauty of Skye but an altogether starker beauty with brilliant colours and stronger light. The trees were thick with birds, screeching and whirling in dizzy circles of green and yellow and red.

'Whatever are they?' she asked.

'Parrots!' said Mr Reekie. 'Parrots and rosellas and lorikeets. Good to look at and good to eat too. Makes a fine dinner you know, a plump roasted parrot.'

'You *eat* them?' exclaimed Morag in horror. 'You kill those lovely birds?'

'Of course we do! Didn't you ever eat sea-birds from the cliffs on Skye?'

'Yes, but they're only ordinary birds. Black and white and brown.'

'Parrots are ordinary enough here! And just wait till you hear the magpies carolling and the kookaburras laughing! This country grows on you, lassie. It seems strange at first but you'll come to love it. You'll call it "home" one day!'

Morag looked up at her mother. Effie MacDonald was looking around at the bush with wary eyes, frowning a little at the sun's glare and at the unfamiliar colours and sounds and scents. Clearly this place didn't seem anything like home to her! She was riding along on the dray in a daze of bewilderment. Morag could understand how her mother was feeling and yet she was oddly stirred by this new place, this unknown country of red earth and vivid sky, golden birds and a carpet of flowers.

'I could even begin to like it,' she thought to herself in surprise.

'We'll be camping by the westerly turn tonight,' said Mr Reekie. 'There's always a crowd there. We'll be safe from bushrangers if we stick with the crowd.'

Morag glanced at Allan. He raised his eyebrows in his bruised face. Bushrangers! He shrugged his shoulders.

At the end of the day, Danny O'Hara turned his bullocks off the track onto a wide stretch of brown grass where other groups of travellers were already settling in for the night. Camp-fires were burning up brightly under the trees and there was a good smell of cooking meat and woody smoke. A clean water-hole lay close by. Mr Reekie chose his spot carefully under a thick clump of wattles for shelter and not too near any of the diggers' camps. As Danny O'Hara unyoked the bullocks, Mr Reekie called out to Allan and Ewen.

'Come on, you lads. The first thing is to get a camp-fire going. I'll show you how to do it. You girls come too. Everyone who's going to live in the bush needs to know how to make a decent fire.'

They all ran to help. Mr Reekie set them to work

gathering dry leaves and twigs and sticks. He built a neat pyramid and lit it with a scrap of tinder from his box and one strike of his flint on the steel. First a thin trickle of smoke came from the leaves and then a flame.

'Now we pile on the timber!' cried Mr Reekie, as excited as if it were his own first camp-fire. 'Small stuff first and then bigger. Run off and find it now! Make sure it's dry! And don't go out of sight. Just keep your eye on this dray and you won't get lost!'

Morag ran with the rest and hurried back to the fire, her arms full of dry sticks. Meanwhile Effie and the other women were spreading blankets underneath the dray to make their sleeping place for the night. They hung more blankets to act as curtains. They wanted some privacy in this camp where so many men were gathering off the track.

When the fire was blazing and the huge billy of water had been hung over the flames, Mr Reekie unhooked yet another cooked leg of mutton from the end of the dray and set to work with his carving knife.

'Mutton again, I'm afraid,' he announced in mock-gloom. 'Most meals in this Colony are mutton and tea.'

Donald MacDonald and Alec Matheson looked at each other in amazement. There seemed to be an endless supply of good meat in this place at the end of the world.

'But there's no peats, Donald,' muttered Alec. 'I've been looking everywhere but not a scrap of peat for cutting can I see. However do they keep warm in the winter if there's no peats to burn?'

Donald MacDonald pointed to the roaring fire.

'Wood!' he said simply. 'There are so many trees in this place, Alec, they're never short of timber to burn.'

'Wood doesn't smell quite the same as the old peats did,' said Alec sadly but Morag already knew she loved that scent of burning wood.

Now Mr Reekie gathered his people around the fire. He dished out the cold mutton while Allan filled the pannikins with tea. Darkness had fallen. Night came down so quickly in the Colony with no long twilight. Morag glanced over her shoulder at the other glowing fires, the other circles of travellers. From the noisiest group came a burst of song.

> *Cheerily men and heave away,*
> *Heave away, O heave away,*
> *Cheerily men and heave away,*
> *We're outward bound in the morning.*
>
> *O the ocean's wide and the wind blows strong,*
> *And we're outward bound with a merry song.*
>
> *Cheerily men and heave away,*
> *Heave away, O heave away,*
> *Cheerily men and heave away,*
> *We're outward bound in the morning.*

'Allan!' said Morag quietly. 'Do you hear that song?'

'What about it?'

'We've heard it before! Don't you remember? On the ship! The seamen used to sing it while they worked.'

'There are lots of sailors on this track,' said Allan. 'Running off to the diggings. All sailors sing those songs.'

'But that voice, Allan! Listen!'

One powerful voice rose above all the others at the sailors' fire. The tune had changed now.

> *Oh I left my wife in Greenock,*
> *And I sailed across the sea,*
> *And I met a bonny mermaid,*
> *Who said she'd marry me.*
>
> *So I wed my bonny mermaid,*
> *And she took me down below,*
> *Where the water's green and glassy,*
> *And the bluebells never grow.*

'It's the Bosun himself!' gasped Allan. 'From the *Georgiana*! I'd know that voice anywhere!'

'They must be the sailors from our ship,' said Morag. 'The mutineers! You'd think they would've reached the diggings by now.'

'Perhaps they hid up in the hills near Geelong for a while before they made a run for it. They're off to Ballarat.'

'Can you see them properly, Allan? How many are there?'

Allan turned his head cautiously.

'Six, I think. Or seven. I can't quite see through the smoke.'

'But there were many more than that in the mutiny,' said Morag. 'There were seventeen of them, at least.'

'They probably didn't stick together. They'd have more chance of escaping in small groups. Perhaps some of them have been caught.'

'Is Jimmy there, Allan? Can you see him?'

'Morag! I think he *is* there! One of those sailors isn't singing. He's just hunched up near the fire. He looks very like Jimmy to me!'

Now Morag turned her head. She gazed at the circle of raucous sailors. Allan was right! She was sure of it. The hunched young sailor with his fair head right down on his knees was surely Jimmy MacLean!

'How can we talk to him?' she whispered.

'We can't! Just keep quiet about it, Morag. Say nothing to anyone. Forget about Jimmy MacLean. We don't want any trouble.'

Morag nodded but she knew she wasn't going to forget about Jimmy. Somehow or other, in the darkness of this very night, she'd find a way to reach him.

When the meal was finished Mr Reekie and Danny O'Hara took out their pipes and leaned back by the fire for a smoke. Donald MacDonald and the other men joined them, each one bringing out a much-loved clay pipe from pouch or pocket. Then Janet Matheson found her own pipe and stuffed it with a plug of tobacco. She took a glowing twig from the fire and held it to her pipe. Soon she was puffing away with a smile of pleasure on her face. Mr Reekie frowned as he watched her smoking so contentedly amongst the men. He turned his eyes back to the fire and began telling a yarn about his very first year in the Colony, twenty years before. Janet puffed on till the yarn was done.

Meanwhile the older boys had stretched themselves out on plaids under the wattle trees and the women and girls and the younger children had crept under the dray, pulled down the curtain of blankets that hung all the way round, and settled themselves for the night. It wasn't long before Janet crawled in beside them and fell asleep. Morag could still hear the men talking quietly together by the fire for another half hour or so and then she heard them move under the trees to sleep. Alasdair Nicolson was among them. He'd refused Mr Reekie's offer of a bedding for himself and his new wife under a separate tree. They'd wait till they reached *Brolga Marsh*, he'd said quickly.

The night was dry. The sailors' singing had stopped and silence fell on the camping place by the water-hole. The only sounds were the croak of a frog and the hoot of a strange night-bird calling 'Mopoke!' from the trees. Deliberately Morag kept her eyes open in the darkness, willing herself to stay awake. She waited a full hour before she moved.

First she lifted the blanket hanging beside her and looked out into the night. The moon hadn't risen yet. Only the stars blazed down from a black sky and only the smouldering remains of a dozen fires gave any light at all. That suited Morag well. She didn't want light. Her plan would work best in the dark.

She'd been careful to choose a sleeping place on the very outside edge of the long row of bodies under the dray.

From that position it was easy to roll sideways out into the open and to lower the curtain behind her. Now she started to crawl quietly towards the sailors who lay in a wide circle round their fire, their feet towards the centre. Her hands and knees moved over dry twigs and grass. As she came close to the sleeping sailors she looked carefully at each face in turn. It was easy to see which one was Jimmy. Six of the men had thick beards. Only Jimmy's chin and lip were bare, apart from that first downy growth of hair. He was only fifteen, after all.

Morag crept to his head and put her left hand lightly over his mouth to muffle any cry. Then she pressed one finger of her right hand against the waking point by his ear. Jimmy didn't make a sound. He simply opened his eyes and looked up at Morag in disbelief. He shut his eyes tight for a second and opened them again. She was still there! He put out one hand and touched her arm.

'Morag!' he gasped softly, under her hand.

'Come!' she whispered right into his ear.

Morag set off to crawl back across the stretch of ground between the sailors' fire and the dray. Jimmy crawled behind her. She paused by the dray and turned to speak to him.

'Do you want to stay with those sailors?' she whispered.

'No! I want to get back to my ship! But the sailmaker says everyone thinks I was part of the mutiny so I'm too scared to run off on my own. I'd be arrested if I showed my face back in Geelong.'

'I'll talk to Mr Reekie in the morning,' said Morag. 'He'll help you. For the rest of the night you'd better sleep under the dray. It's really for the women and children but there's room at the far end. I'll cover you with a plaid. Keep it over your head and no one'll notice you. Be sure you lie still in the morning till the sailors have gone!'

'They like to start early.'

'Good! Come on! Follow me!'

They crawled the length of the dray and Morag lifted the curtain.

'Creep in here,' she said.

Jimmy rolled under the edge of the dray and lay motionless on a grey blanket. Morag pulled a plaid up over his head and right down to the soles of his bare feet. Only his mouth and nose were left uncovered. She lowered the curtain and crawled back to her own end of the dray. In a few minutes she was asleep with a smile of triumph on her face.

Early the next morning, just as three plump kookaburras were laughing merrily from a branch overhead, Morag woke suddenly and went to look for Mr Reekie. She wanted to be sure to tell him about Jimmy before the sailors starting making a hullabaloo about his escape. He wasn't lying with the other men and boys under the trees but then she saw him a little way off from the camp, crouching down to wash his face in the water-hole. She came closer.

'Mr Reekie!' she called quietly.

He looked up and propped himself back on his heels. His brown face was running with water. He held a block of yellow soap in his hands.

'What's the matter, lassie?' he said.

'I want to talk to you, please, Mr Reekie. It's about Jimmy MacLean from our ship. You see, he wasn't part of that mutiny at all.'

'What on earth are you talking about? I don't know any Jimmy MacLean? Who is he?'

Morag squatted down beside Mr Reekie and told him the whole story of Jimmy Maclean and the mutiny and how Jimmy was forced to leave the ship by the other seamen.

'And some of the sailors are camped just over there,' she concluded, pointing to the still-sleeping circle of men. 'And Jimmy was with them. So I woke him up in the night and I hid him under the dray.'

Morag took a huge breath before she went on.

'Mr Reekie. Please let him come with us to *Brolga Marsh!* He'd be a good worker for you. Or could you help him to get back to his ship? Once Captain Murray knows Jimmy had nothing to do with the mutiny, he'll be sure to take him back on the *Georgiana*. And please, don't tell those sailors that Jimmy's under our dray!'

Mr Reekie didn't answer for a long minute. He dipped his fingers down into the water and rubbed it over his hair and his beard to tidy them.

'It's a strange story, lassie,' he said at last. 'I'd like to help this Jimmy MacLean. I think he'd better come on with us to *Brolga Marsh*. He can work for Mr Martin for a month or two till the dust settles on that mutiny. Perhaps we'll find some way of getting him safely back to his ship again. The *Georgiana* won't be leaving Geelong in a hurry. There'll have to be an inquest and a court case.'

'Thank you!' said Morag. 'I knew you'd help him! I told him you would!'

She threw her arms around Mr Reekie's neck and kissed him on the cheek.

'Now,' he said briskly, pretending not to notice her exuberance, 'the main thing is to keep Jimmy from being discovered. I'll have a word with those sailors when they wake up. I'll tell them I know just who they are. I'll say the troopers from Geelong are hot on their trail. That should send them on their way to Ballarat! You make sure the women leave Jimmy undisturbed till we're ready to go. And keep those curtains hanging down!'

Morag nodded. She hurried back to the dray and started waking the women, one by one, and then the children, to tell them in whispers that Jimmy MacLean was there amongst them, hidden under a woollen plaid. They all sat up in alarm and stared at the long brown bundle at the end of the row but no one said a word. They crawled into the sunlight, shaking and patting the crushed clothes they wore day and night on the track. Soon the sailors were awake.

'Jimmy MacLean! Where are you?' roared the Bosun.

'Come on boy!' shouted the sailmaker. 'We've got to be moving!'

Mr Reekie strode across to speak with them at once. He pointed back down the road they had all travelled and then pointed on towards Ballarat. He had a look of urgent concern on his face and he spoke fast. The sailors didn't wait to argue. In a few minutes they had rolled up their swags, kicked out the fire, and set off at a smart pace along the track to the diggings, glancing back over their shoulders now and then to see if the troopers were close behind.

Once they were well out of sight, Morag drew Jimmy from under the dray. All the children rushed up to greet him and the men and women came close to talk with him, anxious to find out if he'd been hurt.

'I'm all right!' laughed Jimmy, his blue eyes shining. 'I'm just thankful to have got away from them. They're not a bad lot of men, really, but they were all ready to swear that I was part of that mutiny of theirs.'

Mr Reekie's face was delighted as he listened to Jimmy.

'So you speak the Gaelic, Jimmy MacLean! Do you speak English too?'

'Yes, sir,' said Jimmy, switching at once into English. 'My mother was from the Islands but I grew up in Greenock. My father came from Aberdeen.'

'Aberdeen!' cried Mr Reekie, grasping Jimmy by the hand. 'I'm glad to see you, lad. The younger folk are managing their English a bit better every day but it's slow going with the older ones. I keep wondering what Mr Martin'll make of them! You're just the person we need. Someone to translate for me when we get stuck. How about coming to work for Mr Martin for a few months, just to help these Skye folk settle in. Five pounds a month I'll pay you. That's good money for a boy. And I'll write off to Captain Murray. I know you'll want to go back to your ship when she sails.'

'I'll be glad to come, sir,' said Jimmy.

'Good! Now for some breakfast. Cold mutton again this morning.'

'And a pannikin of tea!' added Morag, smiling happily at Jimmy.

12

The Last Crossing

The bullock-dray swung to the north-west. They'd left the busy northerly road to the diggings now and they were following a narrower, more deeply-rutted track where the gumtrees and yellow wattles pressed closer on each side and hung overhead.

'Kangaroos!' cried Danny O'Hara in glee, pointing with his long whip. 'Hundreds of 'em! Look!'

The crofters gasped. A whole herd of the strange and beautiful creatures were leaping across the track, thrusting off their strong back legs and powerful tails, turning their delicate heads to look warily at the dray with its load.

'Will they hurt us?' cried Flora in alarm.

'Not if you leave them alone,' said Mr Reekie. 'Though an old man kangaroo can be fierce in a fight. Just look at those little joeys in their mothers' pouches. Marvellous idea, that!'

Morag watched in astonishment until the kangaroos had bounded lightly away and disappeared into the bush.

'Will we see them again?' she asked.

'Every day, lassie. They're around us all the time. They eat the grass we need for our sheep as a matter of fact. They're a menace and we have to shoot them. But I love to see them leaping all the same.'

Jimmy MacLean walked close beside O'Hara for an hour or two, fascinated with the great beasts and with the bullocky himself. He tried swinging the long whip over his head but couldn't quite get the knack of making it crack and hiss. Then he turned back to walk with the men and the older boys and girls behind the dray, talking over the mutiny yet again, assuring them that he was really all right in spite of the shock and the rough treatment he'd had. Allan, free of his bandages now and looking almost normal, liked to stick near Jimmy.

'Creek ahead!' called O'Hara and the bullocks seemed to shudder. The heavy animals slipped and slid down a steep bank to the edge of the shallow water but they were reluctant to step in. The bullocky roared and swore and swung his whip until at last the bullocks scrambled over the stones in the bubbling creek. The dray lurched and tipped. The people screamed. And then the bullocks were dragging their load up the slope on the other side.

'Well done, O'Hara!' cried Mr Reekie after each new crossing.

O'Hara knew the names of all these little creeks they came to. He greeted each one like an old familiar enemy. The Warrambine, the Mia Mia, the Kuruc-A-Kuruc, the Little Woady Yaloak.

'They're funny names,' remarked Morag as they came up out of the Kuruc-A-Kuruc, water pouring from the wheels, the crofters clinging desperately to the sacks. She said the word over and over again to herself till it slid more easily off her tongue.

'Kuruc-A-Kuruc, Kuruc-A-Kuruc, Kuruc-A-Kuruc!'

'Blackfellers' names!' said Danny O'Hara.

The sun grew fiercer. Morag's face and neck were burnt to a fiery red. Although they'd had weeks to get used to the sun on the ship, there'd always been some shelter there. Here on the track through the bush there was little shade and every crofter's face was sore and sunburnt. Flies buzzed maddeningly around their heads. They had to learn to keep their hands constantly waving in front of their faces to drive them away. At midday, when they sat down on the ground to eat their dinner, hordes of ants swarmed over their legs. The fiercer ants stung them and red lumps and weals rose up on their skin. Grim-faced lizards scuttled all around them through the heat of the day, darting under logs and running up the trunks of trees. One huge lizard had a blue tongue flicking in and out of its mouth.

'Won't hurt ya!' was Danny O'Hara's refrain. 'Jist look out for the snakes! *They* can hurt ya! Give us a yell if ya see one of them snakes and I'll break his back with me whip!'

In the tall trees around them were always the birds. Morag never ceased to be fascinated by their bright colours and their harsh cries. The trees themselves seemed to be on the move with the constant flutter and swoop of those thousands of brilliant wings.

'What do you really think of this place, Allan?' she asked him suddenly as they stood together one warm day, waiting for the billy to boil and gazing into the bush.

'I don't know,' he said, his hand on Morag's shoulder. 'It's so strange. I think I miss the sea. We were never far from it at home, were we? We're sea people, really. But this bush country is somehow wilder than the sea. I don't understand its ways. We'd be lost if we wandered off this track.'

'I think I quite like the bush,' said Morag slowly, her voice uncertain. 'But it scares me. I love the smell of those leaves and the flowers. But it's all so mysterious.'

'Come on!' called Mr Reekie suddenly. 'It's time you all had some lighter clothes. You look ridiculous in those thick shawls and jackets. That's no way to dress in the bush! Let's open up the slops bag and see what we can find!'

He dragged a bulging sack from the dray and slit it open with his knife. He pulled out armfuls of cheap cotton clothing. Shirts and trousers, skirts and dresses, and a bundle of huge floppy hats.

'Take your pick!' he shouted, scattering the clothes on the dry ground.

Morag was delighted. She grabbed a blue cotton skirt and a blouse to match. She pulled off her heavy things and put on the new ones. All the other children were soon transformed but the older folk stared down suspiciously at the cotton clothes and shook their heads. Janet Matheson pulled her black shawl closer around her shoulders and settled the white mutch back on her hair. She was far too hot. She admitted it. But she wasn't going to cast off one stitch of the thick warm clothes.

'Well, just stay as you are!' laughed Mr Reekie good-naturedly.

Flora was dancing around the dray and the standing bullocks. She wore a red cotton skirt that came only half way down her legs and a shirt with short sleeves. Her broad shady hat was a couple of sizes too big for her and almost covered her eyes but she didn't care. She twirled this way and that, making the light skirt fly out in a circle around her knees.

'She'll go a long way, that wee lassie of yours, Donald MacDonald!' said Mr Reekie. 'What fine red hair she has under that hat. She's a beauty!'

Donald watched Flora with new pride. Morag herself felt marvellously light and airy in her new skirt. The touch of the cotton was quite different from the wool against her skin.

That day, for the first time, they ate wild duck shot down with Mr Reekie's gun and roasted over the fire. Danny O'Hara baked a flat round bannock of flour and water in the hot ashes.

'Damper!' he said, breaking off chunks of the fresh bread and passing them around. 'Blackfellers' food.'

'Blackfellows!' cried Morag. 'I saw them back along that diggings track. Who are they, Mr Reekie?'

'They lived here before we came,' he said. 'It was their

country, really. Till we bought it from them for a few sticks of tobacco and some coloured beads. They've had a hard time since the white folk came. Some of the settlers treat them badly – shoot them, break up their camps, take their women. And then they catch our measles and smallpox and they die in hundreds. But Mr Martin treats them well. He's a white man in a hundred, our Mr Martin. He knows those blacks make marvellous stockmen. We've got a whole camp of them by the creek at *Brolga Marsh*.'

'Will they hurt us?' she asked.

Mr Reekie shook his head.

'Not if you treat them right. We've had no trouble at *Brolga Marsh*. Just wait till you meet Tommy Bruk-Bruk! Tommy's my best stockman. He'll have you riding a horse before you know where you are.'

Morag wasn't at all sure that she wanted to ride a horse but she was curious about Tommy Bruk-Bruk.

'Does he have any children? Like us?'

'Lots of them. Mr Martin sent one of Tommy's older girls off to the Mission School last year. She'd be about your age, lassie. Thirteen or thereabouts. But she ran back home after six months. Found the way all by herself. She was too homesick at the Mission but she was there long enough to learn some good English. She's very quick, that girl.'

'What's her name?' asked Morag.

'Kal-Kal. It means cicada, Tommy tells me. You'll hear the cicadas making a racket up in the trees when the summer really comes.'

'Do they belong to the Free Church?' asked Donald, a touch of suspicion in his kindly voice. 'These black people?'

Mr Reekie shook his head and laughed.

'Not to the Free Church. Not to any church. They've got their own beliefs. But Kal-Kal picked up a smattering at the Mission. She sings lots of hymns, anyway.'

'Hymns!' sniffed Donald MacDonald. 'It's the good Gaelic Psalms they'll be needing!'

Five days after they'd left Geelong, Mr Reekie looked up frowning at a morning sky that had turned dull and threatening.

'O'Hara!' he shouted. 'There's rain coming. Hurry those beasts along. We've got to get over the Woady Yaloak before the weather breaks.'

O'Hara shook his head gloomily.

'We'll be too late!' he said. But he let fly at his team with a new torrent of curses.

Rain began falling before midday. First a few heavy drops. Then a steady relentless downpour. Mr Reekie called a halt.

'Tarpaulin!' he yelled. 'We must cover the stores! Quick! Lend us a hand here!'

Everyone ran to help as Mr Reekie dragged a huge grey tarpaulin from the load and began to unroll its heavy folds. The men grasped it around the edges and eased it up over the sacks on the dray and tied it down firmly at the corners.

'On we go, O'Hara!' cried Mr Reekie. 'Only a few miles to the river!'

The rain came down in sheets. The crofters were well used to rain on Skye but never rain like this. They could see nothing ahead or behind them. Even the trees were hidden. They were soaked to the skin. Their faces were running with water. Their boots squelched. Morag took hers off and walked bare-foot again as she'd always done at home. Mud oozed between her toes with every step.

'I'll ride on ahead and see how the river's running!' shouted Mr Reekie and cantered off into the rain. What if he never comes back, Morag wondered.

He was back sooner than she'd expected. Galloping.

'The Woady's running a banker!' he cried. 'Come on, O'Hara! Swing your whip, man, or we'll never make it!'

The bullocks and the dripping people pushed on through

the rain, splashing and slipping on the track that was stream-
ing like a creek under their feet.

'Keep moving!' shouted Mr Reekie, his voice cracking.

At last they came to the river. The Woady Yaloak. They
were too late.

The river followed a crazy zig-zag course down in a
deep gully. River-red-gums grew thickly along the steep
sides and hung over the swirling water. There was no hope
of getting across. The ford was already deep in an angry
yellow torrent, erupting in foam and surging high up the
banks. Logs were whirled along in its path. Morag stood
with Allan and Jimmy on the bank and looked down. A
young kangaroo was struggling helplessly in the middle of
the stream. His feet scrabbled, his head turned and stretched
but he couldn't save himself. The powerful river swept him
swiftly past till he was out of sight around the next bend.
Morag shivered in fear.

'We're not going to try to get over, are we?' she asked
Mr Reekie.

He shook his head.

'We'd be mad to try. Nothing to do but sit it out. We'll
have to stop here. Everyone can get under the dray. No
point lighting a fire just yet. We'll have to eat that cold
damper left over from breakfast.'

O'Hara's bullocks pulled the dray under the thin shelter
of some stringybarks. He unyoked his beasts and hobbled
them nearby. The families huddled together under the dray
in their wet clothes, looking out at the rain and listening
to the roaring river.

'How long will we have to sit here?' Morag asked.

'It could be a week,' said Danny O'Hara grimly.

Morag groaned. She felt trapped in a cave of rain.

'We never should've come!' murmured her mother,
holding tight to little Katie who was coughing and crying
in her arms.

'She's sick!' announced Morag, her hand on the baby's burning forehead. Katie's plaintive cry went on and on.

Two days passed under the dray. There was only cold damper to eat. At the end of the second day the rain stopped as suddenly as it had begun. The trees appeared again out of the dusk like ghosts.

'Can we go across now?' asked Allan, crawling stiffly out of the shelter and standing to look down in horror at the raging river.

'Not a hope!' said Mr Reekie. 'We'll have to wait for the water to go down. What we need now's a decent fire.'

He tried again and again to get his fire going but the leaves under the bark were too damp and the spark from his flint too brief.

'Boss!' called a sudden voice from the trees.

Everyone jumped. Mr Reekie's head jerked up.

'Tommy Bruk-Bruk!' he cried in delight. 'Where are you? Show yourself, man!'

A wet black man stepped out of the shadows. He had a thin band of twisted possum hair around his head and a girdle of fur around his waist with a scrap of dirty red cloth dangling down in front. A cloak of kangaroo fur, the skin side out to keep off the rain, hung from his shoulders and his bare chest was marked in a criss-cross pattern of old scars. He was smiling a broad white smile.

'Plenty bad river, Boss!' said the man, still smiling. 'Plenty bad rain!'

'You're right enough, Tommy. Plenty bad rain! We'll just have to sit here and wait for the water to go down. Could be days!'

Tommy pointed north.

'Better cross up-river, Boss. Molonghip. Better place.'

'Up-river? Beyond Mount Erip? But we never go that way. We always cross here.'

'Morningtime come, I show you, Boss,' said Tommy. 'Now we make fire.'

'It's hopeless,' said Mr Reekie, looking down at his damp hoard of leaves and bark. 'I've been trying for an hour.'

Morag never quite saw just what Tommy Bruk-Bruk did when he bent over the leaves and the bark with a stick that he twirled against a flat piece of wood but in five minutes a wisp of smoke was curling up from the leaves and in ten minutes there was a yellow flame. He fed the flame with leaves, one by one, and then with sticks.

'Now we fill billy, Boss. Make plenty hot tea. Piccaninnies stop jabber-jabber.'

The tea was made. New damper was baking. The children had all stopped their whimpering except for Katie who still sobbed and shivered.

'This one piccaninny plenty sick!' said Tommy peering in at her as she lay in Effie's arms. 'Morningtime come, we take piccaninny home. Plenty quick.'

The sun shone brightly the next morning but the river still roared. Danny O'Hara had agreed to follow Tommy Bruk-Bruk to the better crossing place further north.

'Right, Tommy!' called Mr Reekie. 'You lead the way.'

Tommy first took them a little way back along the track they had come by and then struck up to the left, due north, straight through the trees. Morag could see no sign of a track. Many weary hours later and past Mount Erip they came to the water again.

'This way, Boss!' called Tommy Bruk-Bruk, showing him a place where the steep river banks had given way to a long gentle slope. But the river itself was still as fierce as ever. It surged over the stones, yellow and sinister.

'Plenty good crossing, Boss!' announced Tommy.

'We'll never get through that, Tommy!' said Mr Reekie. 'The bullocks would be swept off their feet!'

'Morningtime come, river plenty small,' said Tommy confidently.

They made camp for the night and slept under the dray. Katie was less restless now. She lay very still and silent. In the morning Morag ran to look at the river. Tommy Bruk-Bruk had been right. The water was a good bit lower.

The families climbed up onto the dray. Tommy walked first into the river, battling against the powerful force of the water that was soon swirling up to his waist. Next came Danny O'Hara, pulling hard on his front bullocks. They shied and backed on the edge till he coaxed them in. The dray rolled forward with the terrified people clinging to the top of the load, the river thundering beneath them as the bullocks staggered and slipped. Last of all came Mr Reekie on his horse, the white dog stretched safely across the saddle.

'Look!' shrieked Flora, standing up in her place and pointing to the far bank. 'There's big birds running! Funny brown birds!' She laughed in delight.

'Sit down, child!' cried Effie, clutching at Flora's skirt but she was too late.

With a sudden wild cry, Flora slipped from the sacks and hurtled into the water.

'Flora! Flora!' Everyone was shouting her name. The bullocks stopped in mid-stream.

Mr Reekie rode his horse straight after her as she bobbed and whirled away in the current. Tommy Bruk-Bruk turned and threw himself into the raging stream, swimming across a deep hole, wading over the stones. Flora was sinking. Morag was crying.

'Save her! Mr Reekie! Save her!' she sobbed.

Tommy grabbed hold of Flora's arm. He hauled her up out of the water. Mr Reekie bent down from his saddle and heaved her onto the horse. He made for the bank with Tommy leaping beside him, one hand still gripping Flora's arm. The girl lay still.

O'Hara bellowed and the bullocks pulled the dray over the last few yards to the bank. Mr Reekie passed Flora down to Tommy. He laid her carefully on the long wet grass and stroked her white forehead. Effie had jumped from the dray the minute it was out of the water. She ran to Flora, calling back over her shoulder.

'Janet! Janet! You're the one we're needing now. Hurry!'

Janet Matheson ran close behind her. She seized the silent child by her two ankles and tipped her up with her head near the ground. She swung her gently backwards and forwards, crooning her name over and over again, while Effie banged vigorously on the girl's back to send the water out of her lungs.

'Flora! Flora!' sang Janet again.

Flora opened her eyes. She let out a long low moan.

'Put me down!' she gulped. 'Put me down!'

'She's alive!' cried Effie and, as Janet turned the girl the right way up again, Effie hugged her in her arms.

The crofters were laughing and crying at once. They had crossed the river and Flora was safe!

Now the dray moved steadily over the last few miles to *Brolga Marsh*, past the big house at Linton Park half-hidden in its trees, and due west towards the setting sun. Flora slept soundly in warm dry clothes and a nest of blankets on top of the sacks of flour.

'Nearly there!' called Mr Reekie in triumph. 'This is all Mr Martin's land on our right now. You Mathesons can camp at our place for tonight. I'll send you on with O'Hara and the dray in the morning. We've got stores for Mr Adams on board as well as our own. And I'll send Jimmy with you to help you settle in.'

Morag looked up at Janet Matheson. She seemed older somehow and frailer. She looked at Jimmy, running level with the bullocks. She didn't want to let either of them go.

O'Hara turned his team off the track and onto a rough farm road between a pair of tall posts still covered with bark. A board nailed to one of the posts was scrawled with two words in clean white paint. Mr Reekie read the words out loud.

'*Brolga Marsh*!' he announced, sweeping his arms in a great circle as he looked out across the paddocks.

'We're here!' cried Morag. 'We're here at last!'

13

Brolga Marsh

When Mr William Martin of *Brolga Marsh* rode out that evening from the bark stables behind his homestead, he heard the new Highland shepherds and their families before he saw them. A weird singing had broken out from the women perched up on the sacks in their black shawls and white caps and from the men and children plodding wearily behind the dray.

> *O thigibh, seinneamaid do Dhia:*
> *Thigeadh gach neach 'na làth'r;*
> *Do charraig thréin ar slàinte fòs,*
> *Togamaid iolach àrd . . .*
>
> *O come, let us sing to the Lord,*
> *Come let us every one,*
> *A joyful noise make to the Rock*
> *Of our Salvation . . .*

The strange language and the wild plaintive music startled him as he sat on his fine little mare, his long legs dangling almost to the ground. His heart sank at the sight of all those children. So many mouths to feed! What had Bob Reekie been up to in Geelong, he wondered, bringing such a peculiar crowd as this to *Brolga Marsh*? The older boys looked strong enough and so did the men, apart from one poor old grandfather shuffling along with a fiddle in his arms.

'Bob!' Mr Martin shouted to his overseer. 'Whatever is it? That terrible noise?'

Mr Reekie rode up to him.

'Don't be anxious, sir,' he said. 'It's just one of their Psalms in the Gaelic. They're rather religious people, you see, sir. It seems to comfort them to sing like that. But they're a biddable people, sir. They'll give you no trouble at all!'

'I hope you're right, Bob!' said Mr Martin, looking doubtfully at Donald MacDonald's broad stern face and at all the heads of untidy hair that hadn't been washed or brushed since the day they left the ship. When the Psalm was ended he greeted the travellers.

'Welcome to *Brolga Marsh*!' he called out to them pleasantly in his high-pitched, clipped English voice. 'You'd better just camp under the dray for tonight. Tomorrow Bob'll take you to the huts. I'll get Mrs Reekie to send out some food.'

Mr Martin didn't linger. He turned his mare and rode back towards the homestead. Danny O'Hara brought the bullocks to a halt by a drooping sheoak tree.

Morag looked around for Tommy Bruk-Bruk but he'd already slipped away into the gathering darkness. She helped the women make up their beds under the dray for the last time. Mr Reekie soon had the camp-fire burning up brightly in a circle of stones. He put the billy on to boil and sent Allan with Ewen to the back door of the homestead for cold mutton and bread. They brought milk too, in a tin bucket, and a slab of yellow butter.

On the far side of the fire, Janet Matheson was brewing up some strange concoction of her own.

'What is it?' asked Morag, coming round to her and peering into the steaming pot.

'Leaves from this tree here,' murmured Janet. 'The

163

sheoak, Mr Reekie calls it. Tommy Bruk-Bruk pulled me down a handful of those green needles and told me to boil them in water. He says the drink'll be just the thing to make Flora better after her drenching in the river and to make little Katie better too.'

'It might poison them!' said Morag in alarm. The water in Janet's billy had turned an unpleasantly murky shade in the firelight.

Janet shook her head.

'That Tommy Bruk-Bruk's a good man, Morag. He'd never poison our children. He *knows* about plants and leaves.'

'Just the way you did on Skye!' exclaimed Morag.

Janet nodded and smiled.

Flora was the first to fall asleep under the dray that night and in the brilliant sunshine of early morning she did seem surprisingly better. Katie too was lively and alert again, her cheeks pink, her eyes bright. She was running around the dray, chattering to herself in her own baby-language. The sickness had passed. Morag wasn't sure if Janet's greenish mixture had done the trick or just a good night's sleep.

Morag and Allan went exploring with Flora before breakfast. The three of them stood in front of Mr Martin's homestead. It was smaller than they'd expected. Nothing like the big stone house at Talisker. The roof was made of thick sheets of solid bark and the walls of split saplings. A hammock hung from the rafters over the wide verandah and a green vine twined around the post at one corner. Smoke was rising from the broad chimney against the end wall. At that moment a smiling woman in a white apron came around the side of the house with a child of about three in her arms. Mr Reekie walked beside her.

'Dadda! Dadda!' shouted the child, holding out his arms to the big overseer. 'Colin wants Dadda!'

Mr Reekie took the boy from his mother and put him down carefully on the ground.

'This is my own wee Colin,' he said. 'Flora, you'll be the one to take care of him. You can keep an eye on that tiny Katie of yours at the same time. No smacking this child of ours, mind. And no shouting. He's to be brought up gently. Do you understand?'

Flora nodded at the doting father and put out one hand towards Colin. The boy took it willingly and was ready to run and play with her at once. Morag liked the look of Mrs Reekie. She had a kind soft face.

'Hurry along now and have your breakfast,' said Mr Reekie. 'Then we'll get the Mathesons off to *Pittencairn* and I'll take you to your hut.'

Janet Matheson was sitting a little apart from the others, her back against the sheoak tree. Morag ran to join her and the two of them contentedly scraped up the porridge from their plates.

'Morag,' said Janet suddenly. 'Have you ever heard any stories about your great-grandma at Borlin?'

'My *great*-grandma?' said Morag in surprise. 'No, not a thing. But I remember my grandma all right. She taught me the songs.'

'Your grandma learnt those songs from her mother. Your great-grandma. She was my mother's cousin.'

'What about her?'

Janet's voice dropped to a whisper.

'Were you never hearing, Morag, that your great-grandma at Borlin had the gift of the Sight?'

Morag was startled. She shook her head.

'Mother's never said a word about that!'

'The Sight often runs in families,' said Janet. 'Mother to daughter. Father to son. Cousin to cousin. Your great-grandma's Sight came straight to me when she died and now there's a strong feeling in my bones that the gift'll be coming to you before long.'

'Oh no!' cried Morag in horror, tears springing to her eyes as she stared at Janet's old face. 'I don't want it!

Please give it to someone else, Janet. Allan could have it!'

Janet laughed.

'The Sight's not mine to give, child. It comes of its own accord and nothing can stop it. I just think it might be coming to you. You've got the right temperament.'

'What's temperament? I don't think I've got one.'

'It's to do with the way you feel things.'

'Oh, then I'm sure I've got quite the wrong temperament, Janet! I feel things far too much! I shriek with fear when I'm scared and I cry when I'm sad and I laugh out loud when I'm happy!'

'That's just the *right* kind of temperament, my little Morag,' said Janet, smiling at her. 'I'm exactly the same. It's because you feel things too much that you might well have the Sight.'

'But how will I know?' asked Morag, still alarmed. 'How will I know if it comes?' She thought of all the terrible stories she'd ever heard about those folk on Skye who'd had the Second Sight. They could foresee death and disaster. They saw funerals passing by, weeks before they really happened. They saw neighbours wrapped up to the neck in their shrouds. They met ghosts from the past. Sometimes they even saw the quiet folk, the fairies, playing about on their green mounds in the broad light of day. Morag didn't want a burden like that!'

'If the Sight ever comes to you, child, you'll know well enough. And it's not all bad, remember. I've seen some grim things in my time but I've had happy moments too with the gift. One winter's night, I was sitting alone in the dark on a cold stone near Loch Brittle. I was just resting on my way home to Talisker. Suddenly a woman came out of the darkness and sat down beside me. I couldn't see her at all. It was pitch black with no moon or stars. But I could hear her and I knew she was there. I wasn't frightened. The woman spoke to me and I liked her voice.

"You don't know who I am, Janet Matheson," she said to me.

"Oh yes I do!" I answered her, though I don't know where the words came from. "You're my cousin, Mairi Campbell, from the Isle of Soay! The cousin I've never met in all my life!"

"You're right indeed, Janet Matheson," she answered me. "You must have the Sight or you never could have known me."

"But how did *you* know *me*, Mairi Campbell?" I asked her. "Sitting here as I am on a stone in the dark?"

"I have the gift too!" she said. "The gift of the Sight!"

So the two of us sat there in the night and we had a fine talk about the strange things we'd seen in our day. Then she walked on to Loch Scavaig and I came home to Talisker. That was forty years ago, Morag. I never saw her again.'

'Was she a ghost, Janet?' asked Morag, a shiver at the back of her neck.

'No, she wasn't a ghost,' laughed Janet. 'It really was Mairi Campbell. She's alive and well on Soay to this very day. The Sight brought us together.'

Morag was silent. She didn't want the Sight but she knew that if it was coming to her she'd have to accept it. The Sight was a gift from God. Or perhaps from the fairies. Who could tell?

There was much hugging and crying and kissing before the three generations of Mathesons climbed onto the dray and rolled away to *Pittencairn*. Jimmy MacLean went along too, to help them through their first few weeks. Janet promised they'd all be back on New Year's Eve if Mr Adams would let them come.

'That's only two months off,' she called down from the dray as the bullocks started to move.

Morag kept her eyes on Janet's white cap and Jimmy's waving hand until the dray was out of sight. She felt strangely troubled.

'Now for the huts!' cried Mr Reekie. 'I'll take you MacDonalds along first. The Nicolsons' hut is a few miles to the north and they'll need to use the pack horse. Come on, Donald, call your family together and pick up those bundles.'

Donald MacDonald hoisted the foot-plough onto his shoulder. Allan lifted the heavy wooden box. Morag took up little Katie. Effie grabbed two bundles of clothes. Mr Reekie strode ahead with Flora skipping on one side and Kenny on the other. He skirted around Mr Martin's homestead, then past his own house and on through a patch of dense scrub. Suddenly they came to the hut, hidden among the gumtrees.

'There we are!' cried Mr Reekie. 'Best shepherd's hut west of Ballarat!'

The family stared at their new home. To Morag's surprise, it was not so very different from the old black house on Skye but these walls were built from upright slabs of timber and the roof was of bark, not turf. Even the chimney, slapped onto the end wall, was of bark. The only door was half way down the long side and two glassless windows were covered with green gauze to keep out flies and mosquitoes.

Mr Reekie pushed open the creaking door. It was dark inside and the air smelt foul. Morag blinked her eyes until she could see. They were standing in the main room. This was clearly the place for living and cooking and eating. The table was a thick sheet of bark nailed to four stumps. The only stools were logs. In the fireplace at the far end lay the ashes of an old fire. Through a doorway to their left, in the second room, Morag saw four bunks of slatted timber. The walls were rough with splinters. The black floor was solid earth.

'It's just like home!' cried Kenny in delight. 'But where will the cow sleep?'

'Cows live outside here,' laughed Mr Reekie. He sniffed

the stale air with distaste. 'You'll need to give the place a good sweep. That last shepherd was a filthy fellow!'

'And the croft, Mr Reekie?' asked Donald, looking out through the doorway at the trees.

'Yes, yes. You can have a whole acre here for your croft. Mr Martin's a generous man. You'll have to fell those gums yourself and grub up the roots and dig the whole patch over in your spare time. You'll need a fence too. All that could take you six months or maybe a year. I'll sell you seed and potatoes for planting when you're ready.'

When Mr Reekie had gone, Donald led his family outside. He plunged his hand into the pouch at his waist and brought out the precious black earth from Talisker. Solemnly he scattered it onto their new croft. It mingled with the fallen gum-nuts and the narrow leaves, with the yellow balls of wattle blossom and with the ancient land itself.

'Unwrap the Good Book, Effie!' cried Donald with tears in his eyes. 'Before we do another thing we'll stand out here on our croft and we'll put up a prayer of thanksgiving to the Lord God who's brought us safely to this new home.'

Under the trees, Donald read slowly in Gaelic from the book of Joshua.

And ye went over Jordan and came unto Jericho . . . And I have given you a land for which ye did not labour . . . For the Lord our God, he it is that brought us up . . . out of the land of Egypt, from the house of bondage and which did those great signs in our sight, and preserved us in all the way wherein we went . . . Therefore we also will serve the Lord; for he is our God.

Morag listened more patiently than usual to her father's long prayer. He went right back to the leaving of Skye, the long voyage, the journey through the bush, the crossing of the rivers and now, at last, this safe arrival, at *Brolga Marsh.*

She liked the bit about the rivers best. That flooded Woady Yaloak had been their very own Jordan!

'I feel like dancing!' she cried when the prayer had ended. She was hopping about from one foot to the other with unexpected happiness.

'Why not?' said Effie, 'Let's dance this very minute!'

Effie stretched out her two hands to Donald. He smiled and took them in his. Allan seized Morag by one hand and Kenny by the other. Flora held Katie in her arms. Whirling and laughing, they all danced right around the hut and stopped breathless at the front door.

'I want a top bunk!' shrieked Kenny, darting into the hut to claim the bed he was to share with Allan, high up near the roof of bark.

Kenny was the one to seize a twig-broom he found in a corner and to sweep the two rooms, shooting the dirt out of the door. Allan and Morag cleared away the old ashes, built a new fire and set it alight. Effie unrolled the blankets onto the beds and put her cooking pots by the fire. She hung their clothes from hooks on the wall and put the Bible high on a shelf, the Waterloo medal still safe between its pages. Donald himself couldn't resist the temptation to turn the very first sod on his croft. He pushed the foot-plough deep into the earth and levered up the rich black soil.

'That'll grow a good crop of potatoes one day,' he said in triumph to Effie who'd come out to watch him. He put his arm around her waist and kissed her on the cheek.

'Water,' she said briskly. 'We need water, Donald.'

He searched in a wide radius around the hut and soon came across a fast little channel, rushing on its way to join Mount Emu Creek. Effie and Morag filled their largest cooking pot and set it on the fire.

Within two hours, Mr Reekie had taken the Nicolsons to their hut at the out-station and was back again.

'Come on!' he called. 'I want to show you the sheep-run from a little hill behind the homestead. You need to know the lie of the land.'

He led the MacDonalds back through the scrub and up to the top of a steep grassy knoll. Whichever way they looked they could see mile upon mile of open plain, dotted with huge trees and cut by narrow winding creeks.

'Mr Martin's got twenty thousand acres here,' he said proudly, 'and twenty thousand sheep. There's a small herd of cattle as well. Mainly milkers.'

Allan gasped. Twenty thousand acres and twenty thousand sheep!

'How do you look after so many, sir?' he asked.

'We've got shepherds in their huts at the out-stations all over the run. We've lost some to the diggings but the convicts are still there. They like an isolated life, those old lags. They drink too much but they're good with the sheep. The blacks are good with the cattle.'

Mr Reekie explained how each shepherd had to set off with a flock of six hundred sheep soon after sunrise. He had to walk behind them, tailing them all through the morning and letting them wander and feed till midday. Then he was to turn them round and bring them slowly back to the starting point by sunset. He penned them up behind hurdles for the night and his mate would take over as watchman. The watchman looked after the hut and cooked the meals but at night he lay in a little watchbox near the flock with a gun under his pillow in case of trouble.

'What sort of trouble?' asked Donald warily.

'Dingoes mainly. Or some strange tribe of blacks from right up beyond Mount Emu, looking for easy food. The watchman fires over their heads and they run off. It's easier to hear the dingoes. They howl. The blacks are as silent as the night itself.'

'Does the watchman ever have to kill anyone?' asked Morag, thinking anxiously about Allan with a gun in his hand in the middle of the night. 'He doesn't have to shoot black people like Tommy Bruk-Bruk, does he?'

'No no!' said Mr Reekie quickly. 'Mr Martin won't have any killing! But on some of these sheep-runs the squatters let their shepherds kill off the blacks as if they were dingoes or kangaroos! It's not right! We all kill the dingoes, of course. That's another matter altogether.'

'Dingoes?' said Morag, still unsure what they were.

'Wild dogs,' said Mr Reekie. 'A bit like wolves. They take our lambs if we're not careful.'

Allan and Morag looked at each other with fear in their eyes. Their father quickly changed the subject.

'We were wondering, Mr Reekie, if Mr Martin would give us a day off when the New Year comes round. That's always our great time on Skye.'

'Will you work over Christmas?' asked the overseer cautiously.

'Of course! Free Church folk never bother with Christmas!'

'Right,' said Mr Reekie. 'I'll need every single member of your family at Christmas when the other shepherds get blind drunk. But you'll have two days off for New Year. I can't say fairer than that.'

Donald was satisfied.

'Right, Donald and Allan,' said Mr Reekie. 'You'll start work tomorrow morning. One flock each. Effie, you're the hutkeeper but you'll help with the milking and work in the dairy as well. Morag, you'll go to the homestead and learn from my wife. As for watching at night, you'll just have to take it in turns. Young Kenny there can help you, Donald. He'll make a fine shepherd in a year or two.'

Mr Reekie strode away down the hill. The family stood there, looking out with bewildered eyes at the vast grassy paddocks of *Brolga Marsh*. Mr Martin's sheep-run stretched all the way to a distant horizon and then still further, brown and green under a hot sun.

'It's a strange country!' said Donald at last.
'And a long way from the sea!' said Effie.
'But there's plenty to eat here!' shouted Kenny happily.
Morag couldn't help smiling. All of them were right.

14

Dingoes!

When Morag woke early the next morning, bright light was shining in through the cracks between the slabs of the hut. She remembered with a pang that the Mathesons and Jimmy were miles away at Mr Adams' sheep-run and the Nicolsons miles away at the out-station. Rory MacRae was far off in Van Diemen's Land. She missed them all.

She climbed out of her lower bunk, careful not to wake Katie at the other end, and ran into the main room of the hut. Last night's fire was still smouldering and the air was full of smoke. Morag opened the door. A black girl sat there, waiting. She wore a shapeless blue cotton dress with short sleeves. Her legs and feet were bare.

'Hullo,' said the girl eagerly with a gleaming smile. 'I can speak your language, you know! I learnt English at the Mission School. I was the best in the whole class!'

Morag smiled back.

'It's not really my language,' she explained. 'We speak the Gaelic. But I did learn some English on the ship.'

'I thought you came from the English-country,' said the girl, disappointed. 'My teacher at the Mission School came from the English-country.'

Morag shook her head.

'No, we come from Skye,' she said.

The black girl looked puzzled. She tipped back her head and gazed up at the immense arc of blue above them.

'From the sky?' she asked, her voice awed and almost frightened. 'You come from the sky?'

'No, no!' laughed Morag, stepping right out from the doorway now and into the brilliant sunshine. She squatted down on the ground beside the girl. 'Not from the sky up there! From the Isle of Skye. It's an island in the sea, far away from here. In Scotland.'

'I've heard about the sea,' said the girl, full of new confidence. 'My teacher at the Mission School told us it was like a big, big lake.'

Morag nodded. The sea was much more than a big lake but she couldn't find the words to describe it.

'Do you live here? At *Brolga Marsh*?' she asked the girl.

'Yes. At our camp. It's not far away. Just down there by the creek.' And she pointed away through the trees. 'My father works for Boss and Big Boss,' the girl went on. 'They call my father Tommy but his real name's Bruk-Bruk. My teacher at the Mission School used to call me Daisy but my real name's Kal-Kal. You can call me Daisy if you want to.'

'I like your real name better,' said Morag. 'And I know your father already. He helped us on the track when the rain came down. What does his name mean? Bruk-Bruk?'

'It's a tree. Boss calls it the sheoak. My father was born under one of those trees. My grandma told me she stood with her back against the trunk and then he was born. That's why she gave him the name.

'I used to have a grandma too,' said Morag, sadly. 'But she's dead now. She taught me all the old songs and the old stories.'

Kal-Kal looked astonished.

'So did mine!' she said. 'I didn't know white people had old songs and old stories. I thought they just had hymns and the Bible.'

'We do have the Bible,' said Morag. 'But we have old

songs and stories as well. Stories about the water-horse and the fairies and the witches.'

'What's the water-horse?' asked Kal-Kal.

Morag looked a bit scared. She didn't even like to mention the water-horse. She spoke very quietly.

'We call him the *each uisge* in our own language. He's a horrible kind of huge horse that lives under the water in our rivers. And sometimes he comes out and changes into a young man. And he finds a beautiful girl and he says he loves her and he asks her to marry him and he promises her all sorts of wonderful things. And if she says yes then he takes her down into the river and no one ever sees her again.'

'Just like the Bunyip!' cried Kal-Kal in delight and terror. 'Except *he* doesn't promise anything much. He justs grabs people and takes them into the river. My grandma *saw* the Bunyip in our creek once but she ran and she ran and she got safely back to the camp. He didn't ever catch her. But you do have to be careful.'

Morag nodded.

'I could sing you one of our songs,' offered the girl in the blue dress and she began to rock backwards and forwards as she sat there. Her voice rose high in a torrent of strange words that Morag couldn't understand at all. The song went on and on and Kal-Kal smiled happily as she sang.

'That's all about the kangaroo,' she announced at the end.

'I'll sing you one of our songs if you like,' said Morag and she began.

> *Ho ro, my baby, ho ro,*
> *You are the child of the swan,*
> *Ho ro, ho ro.*
>
> *Ho ro, my baby, ho ro,*
> *The swan left you there by the loch,*
> *Ho ro, ho ro . . .*

Soon Kal-Kal was joining in every 'Ho-ro' as if she'd known the song all her life. When it was finished, Kal-Kal stood up. She seized Morag by the hand and led her through the trees and onto the low hillock where Mr Reekie had taken them the day before.

'There's our camp,' said Kal-Kal, pointing to a clump of dome-like huts by the river-red-gums along the creek. Then she turned herself right around in a circle and stretched out her arms to the north, to the south, to the east, to the west.

'This is all our land,' she said. 'It belongs to our tribe. The Wathaurung Tribe.'

'No, it doesn't!' laughed Morag. 'It belongs to Mr Martin. The one you call Big Boss. It's not your land any more.'

Kal-Kal frowned.

'My grandfather was tricked into selling. All he got was tobacco and beads! The white man before Big Boss wanted it for his sheep. But this land still belongs to us and we belong to this land.'

Suddenly Morag understood.

'*We* had to leave our croft on the Isle of Skye because of the sheep!' she said. 'And we don't feel the same since we left.'

'The white man before Big Boss killed my grandfather,' said Kal-Kal sadly. 'He killed my uncle too. Did your Big Boss kill your grandfather?'

'No, no, nothing like that,' said Morag, shocked at the very idea. 'We didn't have any killing. But we had a terrible famine when everyone was hungry.'

At that moment, Morag caught the faint wailing sound of the morning Psalm coming from her hut beyond the trees. Kal-Kal heard it too.

'What is it?' she asked. 'That funny noise?'

'My family's singing the Psalm. I'll have to go now.'

'I'll come too,' said Kal-Kal, not waiting to be asked.

They ran together to the hut. Morag's family was standing in a tight circle in the centre of the main room, their voices crying out as if in anguish. Kal-Kal eased her way into the ring and joined in the tune with smiling enthusiasm though she knew nothing of the words. Donald MacDonald glanced down at her in surprise and raised one reddish eyebrow as he gave out each line but he didn't pause in his singing. After the Bible reading and the prayer, there was a sudden silence as all the MacDonalds gazed at the Aboriginal girl in her short blue dress. She gazed back at them, turning her eyes from face to face.

'I like your funny singing!' she said.

'There's nothing funny about it!' exclaimed Morag's father. 'The sooner you learn those good Psalms, child, the better! Morag here will teach you.'

'Morag!' said Kal-Kal, turning to look at her again. 'Is that your name? I like it.'

'This is Kal-Kal,' Morag explained to her family. 'Tommy Bruk-Bruk's her father.'

They smiled at her. Flora reached out one hand to touch the blue dress.

'The porridge is ready,' said Effie MacDonald, putting a pile of tin plates onto the bark table. 'It's been cooking all night.'

'Don't eat in here!' cried Kal-Kal. 'There's too much smoke and I can still smell that last shepherd. It's better outside. Come on.'

The family followed her obediently outside and sat, as she did, straight down on the ground.

'I think I'll have some of that stuff,' she said, peering into the black pot of thick white porridge and sniffing at it.

Effie found an extra plate. She dished up the porridge and poured on creamy milk from a white jug. Everyone ate.

Suddenly Kal-Kal sprang to her feet.

'Here's Boss!' she cried.

Mr Reekie was hurrying towards the hut with his son Colin running on tiny legs beside him.

'Time to work, everyone!' he shouted. 'We're late! From tomorrow onwards, you'll start at sunrise. Flora, you take wee Colin here and your own little sister. You can play anywhere near Mr Martin's homestead or up on my own verandah, but don't go near the creek. And look out for snakes! Effie, you begin straight away on the milking. Tommy Bruk-Bruk's down in the cowshed already. Daisy, you take Effie MacDonald to your father. Then come back here. Double-quick!'

'Yes, Boss,' said Kal-Kal and she ran off beside Effie who seemed suddenly nervous as she faced her first day's work.

'Donald, you're to take that Kenny of yours and you'll tail the home-flock to the north-west. Make sure you count them out and then count them back in again at the end of the day. Take some bread with you so you won't be hungry. You can have two of the dogs.'

'I'm a shepherd!' Kenny yelled in triumph as he ran off with his father.

'Allan, you'll tail the second flock. You'll walk to the north-east. That way!' He pointed over the plains. 'You can have my own dog Sandy to help you and a couple of the kangaroo dogs.'

'I could go with him, Mr Reekie!' Morag offered suddenly. 'I think I'd sooner be a shepherd like Allan than a housemaid. I'm good with animals.'

'Shepherding's not quite the best thing for girls, lassie. Too lonely. My wife wants to train you for the big house.'

Morag sighed. Mr Reekie relented.

'All right. Take Morag with you just this once, Allan,' he said. 'To keep you company. But tomorrow you'll be on your own.'

Morag collected their bread. With Sandy beside them they followed Mr Reekie to the kennels where a pack of

179

six barking dogs rushed out at them like lightning. Morag cringed back behind Allan. These dogs were nothing like Skerry at home on Skye. They were as big as greyhounds and their coats were oddly mottled and blue.

'Lie down!' bellowed Mr Reekie and the fierce dogs froze at once. They lay panting on the ground, their long tongues hanging out between sharp teeth, their eyes fixed on Mr Reekie.

'Kangaroo dogs, we call them,' he said, bending down to stroke each of their heads in turn. 'They can fly at a kangaroo's throat and bring him down in a minute. But they won't hurt the sheep and they won't hurt you. I'll just teach you the whistles I use with them and you'll have no trouble at all.'

Morag and Allan looked at the dog's cruel mouths and they glanced at each other. But they easily picked up the whistles they'd need and walked off together behind their flock. The animals moved very slowly, cropping the grass as they went, spreading out in a great fan over the paddocks.

'I'm glad you're with me today, Morag,' Allan admitted. 'I'd feel scared on my own with six hundred sheep and those peculiar dogs. I always worked with Father at home.'

'Mr Reekie seems to think you're a man,' said Morag.

'I don't really feel like a man! I just wish Jimmy was here!'

'So do I!' said Morag.

Half an hour later, they came to the Aborigines' camp by the creek. Walking as slowly as the nibbling sheep, Morag and Allan had plenty of time to look and listen. First they saw the low curved huts of bark and leafy boughs and then they heard the loud shouts of laughter, the racket of voices, the barking of a dozen dogs, the cheerful shrieking of children crawling about in the dust. Not a single one of those children had a bright dress like Kal-Kal's. All the Aborigines were stark naked apart from a girdle at their waist. Their black hair was short and matted. Their bodies gleamed in the sunlight. The breasts of the old women sagged low but the young girls' breasts were high and firm. Morag stared.

All the women in that camp were busy. Some were grinding wild seeds between flat stones, some were digging for roots in the earth with a stick, some were weaving mats and bags from reeds, others were poking at the cooking fires or gathering armfuls of wood. The whole place was alive with noise and movement. Morag and Allan edged cautiously past, gazing at the Aborigines with a mixture of fascination and fear.

'Allan, did you know about these black people?' asked Morag. 'When we were still on Skye, I mean.'

Allan shook his head.

'No one said a word about them,' he said.

'Kal-Kal says they really own all this land,' said Morag.

'Not any more, they don't! Mr Martin owns it!'

'Allan, these black people were pushed off their land just the way we were!' said Morag. 'They're exactly like us! They've got old songs and stories too and they've got a language of their own that Boss and Big Boss can't understand at all!'

'But we wear more clothes!' laughed Allan.

They left the camp behind them and moved on through the long hot morning, over the creek and across the wooded plain. They half-closed their eyes against the glare of the sun and waved their hands to ward off the flies. After a midday break for bread, while the sheep were drinking at a water-hole, Allan took out his chanter and played a few tentative notes. Morag watched him as he picked out the old tune they both knew well – 'I will return no more.'

'You're really getting the hang of it, Allan!' she said. 'You'll be a good piper. You'll be as good as those famous MacCrimmons! I do miss the sound of Neil MacKinnon's pipes, don't you?'

'And Alec Matheson's fiddle too,' agreed Allan.

'And Jimmy's sea-songs,' said Morag. 'Whenever Jimmy's around I feel more cheerful. I don't know why it is.'

They turned the flock and wandered slowly back to the homestead. The whole day was so different from a day with the sheep or the cattle on Skye. The grass was a duller green, the trees were a strange untidy shape, the air was dry, the light was brilliant, the birds were startlingly bright and the sky amazingly blue. At the end of the day, when the sheep were safely penned away behind their hurdles, Mr Reekie came to see them at the hut with still more orders.

'We'll put the watchbox between the two flocks and one watchman can listen for them both. Allan, you'll be watchman tonight and your father'll do it tomorrow night. You'll get some sleep in the box but you've got to keep listening, even in your sleep.'

'How can he listen in his sleep?' asked Morag.

'It's a knack. You keep one ear open all through the night.'

Allan frowned. He was tired already from the long day and he wasn't relishing the thought of a night in the watchbox.

'What about the gun?' he said. 'Do I need a gun?'

'Not tonight. You don't know how to handle one yet. I'll just give you a couple of wooden clappers. They'll scare off any marauders. Bang them together and shout and yell. You can have Sandy with you too.'

Allan was still frowning. He didn't seem very sure of himself. His father spoke up for him.

'Mr Reekie, this boy's only young. You can't leave him out in the bush on his own all night! Let me do the watching!'

'No, Donald. The boy has to do a man's job from the start or he's no use to Mr Martin. He'll be safe in the box. Don't coddle him!'

'I'll come with you, Allan,' said Morag quickly. 'Then you won't be scared. I could run to get Father if we have any trouble.'

'I'll come too,' shouted Kenny.

Allan grinned at them both in relief.

'Thanks!' he said. 'Just for the first night. If there's room in the watchbox for three of us.

The watchbox standing between the two quiet flocks looked to Morag like a large coffin on legs. That didn't make her feel any happier about the night ahead. She and Allan and Kenny opened up the door and climbed inside. They wrapped themselves well in their warm plaids and lay down. The dog was at Allan's feet, right by Morag's nose.

'Do we shut that door or leave it open?' she asked.

'We'd better leave it open,' said Allan. 'Then we'll be able to see better by the light of the moon and the stars.'

'I just hope there's nothing to see,' mumbled Morag and she fell asleep at once in the cramped uncomfortable box.

She woke with a start. A terrible long-drawn-out howl from one lone animal's throat filled the night. It seemed like a signal. At once it was answered by other howling voices. Morag shook Allan and Kenny awake and the three of them sat up in the box, straining their eyes to see into the moonlit darkness. The sheep were no longer quiet. They moved restlessly in their vast pens and bleated in fear.

'Dingoes!' whispered Kenny.

Now they could see them. A mob of wild dogs sur-rounded the hurdles of the second flock, tipping back their heads to howl at the moon, snapping and growling at the cowering sheep just beyond their reach.

'The clappers!' cried Morag.

Allan climbed up on top of the watchbox. As he crashed the two wooden clappers together, Morag and Kenny scrambled up beside him and shouted and yelled. The noise was appalling but the dingoes hardly noticed. They howled. They surrounded the flock. They leapt up and down. They pushed against the hurdles.

'Can they jump over?' asked Kenny.

No one knew the answer.

'One of us'll have to go for Mr Reekie,' said Allan.

'Not me!' said Morag quickly.

'I'll go!' said Kenny and he leapt down from the box and ran off before Morag could hold him back. Sandy leapt after him.

'Allan! We shouldn't let him go!' gasped Morag. 'Those dingoes could get him! They'd tear him to bits!'

'He's running past the home-flock,' said Allan. 'The dingoes aren't bothering about those sheep yet. They'll never see him. Look! There he goes! He's running like the wind!'

Allan and Morag kept up their din, banging the clappers and yelling into the night. Without the dog they felt more frightened than ever. Morag was crying as she shouted.

'Look!' she gasped.

From the Aborigines' camp came a sudden forest of burning torches and a blood-curdling roar far more terrible than the noise of the dingoes themselves. With spears or waddies in their right hands and flaming brands in their left, with a pack of kangaroo dogs barking at their heels, the men of the camp came rushing towards the dingoes. Allan stopped his clappers. Morag stopped her shouting. They stood in silence on the box and stared at the dark shapes slipping through the trees. The first spears flew. The dogs leapt at the dingoes. Morag shut her eyes. Now a shot rang out. Mr Reekie was there with his gun. The dingoes fled. Six of them lay dead by the hurdles.

'Plenty bad dingoes!' said the reassuring voice of Tommy Bruk-Bruk close beside them. 'All gone now!'

'You were just in the nick of time, Tommy,' said Mr

Reekie. 'One of those dingoes got right into the flock. We've lost a couple of lambs.'

Morag was crying again. Bellowing and sobbing. Mr Reekie lifted her down from the box.

'I never should've let you stay out here all night. The Missus told me I was wrong. This watchbox is no place for a girl.'

'It's no place for me either!' said Allan stoutly. 'I was just as scared as she was!'

'You'll get used to it, lad,' said Mr Reekie calmly. 'I'll teach you how to use the gun. The dingoes don't come every night, you know. Now all of you get back to your hut. Tommy'll watch for the rest of the night.'

Mr Reekie suddenly burst out laughing, relieved that nothing worse had happened. Tommy Bruk-Bruk laughed with him. All the Aborigines were laughing as they set up the fallen hurdles and dragged away the dead dingoes. Morag and Allan were the only ones who couldn't find a thing to laugh at. They were longing for sleep.

15

New Year's Eve

The rest of the night was all too short. Early in the morning Morag was woken by Kal-Kal's shrill voice calling from outside the hut.

'Morag! Morag! The brolgas are dancing on the swamp! Come and see!'

Morag felt too tired and stiff to move after her hours in the watchbox but she did want to see those birds. She pulled on her skirt and blouse and ran outside.

'What's the swamp?' she asked as she hurried along beside Kal-Kal.

'It's just another name for the marsh. A wet bit of land by the creek where the water overflows. That's the place the brolgas love.'

As they came near to the pools and the reeds, Kal-Kal stopped suddenly by a crooked swamp-gum.

'We'll climb this tree,' she said. 'Then we'll see better but the birds won't see us.'

In an instant, Kal-Kal was gripping the tree-trunk with hands and knees and feet. She was shinning up to sit on a low bough behind a curtain of leaves.

'I can't do that!' laughed Morag, looking up at her.

'Yes, you can! Hitch up your skirt and grip the trunk. It's easy!'

Morag didn't find it easy. She slipped and scrambled. She fell back to the ground. Her hands and legs were scratched and bleeding. Her skirt was torn. Kal-Kal leant down and grabbed her by the arm and heaved her up the last stretch till she sat panting on the branch.

When Morag caught sight of the marsh, she forgot about her stinging cuts and scratches. Never had she seen so many different birds gathered together in one place, not even along the shores of the lochs on Skye. They were wading, swimming, feeding, flying, calling. Pelicans and ibis, cormorants and herons, spoonbills and swans, sandpipers and shovellers. And there at the heart of the swamp were the beautiful brolgas themselves! On long elegant legs, the silvery-grey birds were leaping and dancing, their feet splashing the water, their graceful necks bending and stretching, their wings opening and closing. They stepped forward lightly and they bowed. They lifted their legs up high.

'They really *do* dance!' murmured Morag in amazement. 'It's true!'

Kal-Kal nodded.

Morag gazed on and on, fascinated by the prancing birds, till their courtship dance was finished for the day and their wings folded.

'Time for work!' said Kal-Kal, imitating Mr Reekie's voice exactly and then dropping back into her own voice as she added. 'You'll be starting in the homestead today, Morag, working for the Missus. I'll come with you.' She slid down the tree.

At the back door of the homestead, Kal-Kal knocked. Mrs Reekie smiled as she opened it and led them to the kitchen. Morag's new life began at the moment when she put on the neat white apron Mrs Reekie held out to her. Kal-Kal didn't wait long. Soon she scampered out of the door and back to her camp again. Morag had a long day ahead of her.

She swept floors and polished furniture. She beat mats outside in the dry air. She set tables and washed dishes.

In a ramshackle wash-house beyond the back door, she pummelled clothes on a wash-board over a tub of hot water. She rinsed and wrung the clothes, twisting the long wet bundles in her aching hands. She pegged them out on a line to dry in the warm wind.

In the cool dairy she helped her mother to pour buckets of milk into wide shallow bowls to let the cream rise. She began to learn to make the butter with yesterday's cream, plunging the handle up and down in the churn till the first yellow specks of butter began to come. Time and time again Morag thought longingly of Allan's free outdoor life, as he trudged alone over the plains behind the sheep or sat on a log to play his chanter under the trees. At home on Skye and even on the ship she'd been free to do almost whatever she liked. Now she had to work like a grown woman. She wished she could be a child again.

After the first few weeks, Morag began to tackle her jobs in the homestead with more skill and confidence. Now and then she saw Mr Martin himself. He always nodded to her in a vague and kindly sort of way as if he couldn't quite remember who she was or what she was doing there in his homestead. The squatter spent most of his days at a table on the verandah, reading his books or writing long letters home to England. He left the management of his run entirely to Mr Reekie. Catching sight of Mr Martin working on a letter one day, Morag remembered it was time for her to write to Mr Cameron again. Before anyone else was awake the next morning, she sat outside the hut with her paper resting on a smooth log of wood. There was so much she wanted to tell him.

Dear Mr Cameron,

We are here at our new home in the bush! I wish you could see our hut. It's a bit like our black house at Talisker but it's made of saplings and bark. Allan is a real shepherd now. I think he feels a bit lonely on his own all day with no one to talk to except the dogs. Mr Martin is the landlord here and I'm learning to be a housemaid in his homestead. Our work is much harder than it was on Skye and we're never allowed to sit about doing nothing but the pay is better and the food is good. I have a new friend called Kal-Kal. She is black. Did you know there were lots of black people living here, Mr Cameron? Kal-Kal says this used to be their own country till the white people came and took it.

We had a long journey here in the bullock-dray from Geelong. At first I was scared of the strange bush and all the creeks we had to cross and the lizards and the ants but now I'm getting used to everything. I love the birds and the kangaroos. There's no peat at all here but we burn logs from the bush on our fire. The hut gets very hot with the sun outside and the fire inside.

We have a fine little croft of our own but Father says it will be a long time till we have it ready for planting. Still, the digging makes him happy. I am sorry to have to tell you that there is no Free Church here – no church at all – but we have our own service every Sabbath afternoon under a tree. I like that.

Most of all I miss the sea. Sometimes at night I lie in my bed and try to remember the sound of the sea but all I can hear are the sounds of the bush. Kal-Kal says she loves the bush. I wonder if I'll ever come to love it too.

Mother cries sometimes. She feels homesick for the Island and the sea. But she is very brave. She says she is getting tougher every day. This is a good country for poor people like us, Mr Cameron. In a few more years we might feel at home here at Brolga Marsh, even though we're so far from Skye.

I send my respectful good wishes to you and to Mrs Cameron. Please tell our old friends to think of coming here. They will never be hungry again.

Morag MacDonald

As November moved on into December, the weather grew hotter every day. There was no escaping from the heat. Even Mr Martin on his shady verandah, with his pipe and his whisky at the end of each day, had to fan himself with a book.

Allan and Morag cooled off in the creek. An evening plunge in the bubbling water was soon part of the family's new pattern of living. Not that Donald MacDonald himself was so keen on a dip in the creek. He left that kind of thing to the women and the young ones. Washing his face and hands was enough for him. He wasn't going to change his old ways.

Jimmy had come walking back from the Adams' sheep-run as soon as he'd helped the Mathesons to settle into their hut and learn their tasks. Morag was glad to see him. He made himself so useful to Mr Reekie that the Boss didn't want to part with him. Jimmy took his turn with Donald and Allan at walking behind the sheep all day and lying half-asleep in the watchbox to guard the flocks all night. He cheerfully tackled any odd jobs around the home-stead and the stables. He was good with the horses and soon he could ride. He mended bits of bridle and broken hurdles. He rounded up the cows at milking time. In the evenings, just before dark, he helped Donald to make a start on cutting down the saplings on his croft. Together with all the family they grubbed up the tough roots or burned them slowly out, always with buckets of water ready to douse any spreading flames. Mr Reekie had warned them about the horrors of the bushfires the year before and they knew they had to be careful.

Jimmy slept on a mattress of leaves – bush feathers he called them. He had a small white tent of his own and he ate his meals with the MacDonalds by a tree near their hut. No rain fell in those weeks up to the year's end. The hot wind blew from the north and sometimes a cool change blew from the south but neither wind brought a drop of rain.

'You're a good lad,' Morag was pleased to hear Mr Reekie saying to Jimmy more than once after a hard day's work. She was even more pleased when he added. 'I just wish you'd give up that mad idea of yours of going back to sea. You're wasted on a ship! You should settle down here in the Colony. Work for me for five years, son, and then you'd get a job as overseer anywhere in Victoria!'

But Jimmy always just grinned and shook his head.

'I really do want to get back to my ship, sir,' he said. 'And to Captain Murray. As soon as you hear from him, I'll be off! There's something about the sea. It pulls me back all the time. But I like this life on the land, Mr Reekie, and I know I couldn't find a better boss than you, sir! Not if I searched from one end of the Colony to the other.'

This always delighted Mr Reekie. He would clap Jimmy on the back and call him a good lad yet again. Mr Reekie wasn't the only one who wished Jimmy would stay. Morag begged him to give up the sea but she had no more success than Mr Reekie himself. Jimmy's mind was firm.

'The sea pulls me back, Morag!' was his only answer.

As the evenings grew lighter, Kal-Kal took Morag to see the fish-traps higher up the creek where her father caught eels. She took her to watch great flocks of emus running fast over the plain on their comic spindly legs. She told her stories of the Dreamtime long ago, and about the sun, the moon and the stars, about the spirits that live in the trees, about the spiny ant-eaters, the koalas, and the platypus in the creek, about how everything came to be the way it is.

'Are those stories of yours really true, Kal-Kal?' Morag asked her. When Kal-Kal swore that every word was true, Morag told her own stories of the water-horse, the witch-cat, and the little quiet people who live under the green mounds on the Isle of Skye.

'Are those stories really true?' Kal-Kal asked every time, her eyes wide with excitement.

'My grandma always said they were true and Janet Matheson says so too. You'll see Janet on New Year's Eve and then you can ask her yourself.'

She didn't want to disappoint Kal-Kal by mentioning her father's views about those old stories.

Late one Sunday afternoon in December, Morag was alone by the creek. Mrs Reekie always gave her a half-day's rest on the Sabbath and it was almost time to go back to the hut for the family's evening prayers. She sat right on the edge of the bank, trailing her hot feet in the water that swirled and chattered around the flat grey stones. As she looked across to the thick scrub on the far side of the creek she blinked and blinked again. She was not sure of what she was seeing. She felt an uncomfortable pricking at the back of her neck. She thought she could see four tall Highlanders, their plaids in place but no bonnets on their heads, walking slowly under the trees, two in front and two behind. They were carrying a long box high on their shoulders and steadying it with their hands as they went. Whatever it was, it couldn't have been very heavy. The men walked lightly, not bending at all under the weight. Was that her father in front and Tomas Matheson beside him? No, she was wrong. She didn't recognize the faces at all though the four men had seemed oddly familiar at first. Who were these strange Highlanders wandering about in the bush on Mr Martin's land? She called out to them in the Gaelic but when no reply came back to her she tried the new word she'd learnt in the Colony.

'Coo-eee! Coo-eee!'

The four men walked steadily on. Not one of them even turned to look at her. Morag blinked again and when she opened her eyes they had gone. She shook her head and leant over to splash her face with water. She stared across the creek. There was no sign at all now of anyone walking through the bush. Had she imagined it, she wondered? She leapt up in fright and ran on bare feet back to the hut. Just as she was about to tell her mother, something stopped her. Some instinct warned her it would be better not to speak at all of the four tall men she thought she had seen. She tried to forget them. In fact she did forget them altogether until New Year's Eve came at last and that was the day when the memory flashed back into her mind.

'I'll ask Janet Matheson,' she said to herself in a rush of relief. 'She'll be here tonight with all the rest of her family and I'll ask her about it then. I suppose it was just the terrible heat made me see a kind of mirage through the trees.'

The Nicolsons were the first to arrive at *Brolga Marsh* on New Year's Eve, trudging in from their out-station six miles to the north. They came in the early afternoon. Alasdair Nicolson was carrying his older girl on his back; Ewen carried the little one. Calum and Kirsty were brown from the sun and Morag thought they even seemed to have grown taller in the weeks since she'd seen them last. Kirsty's cough had gone. Mistress Shona Nicolson was more at ease with her new husband Alasdair now. She was not so stiff. The two families had melded comfortably into one.

Morag and Allan rushed to greet their old friends. Effie MacDonald flung her arms around Shona. Everyone was laughing and crying at once. They sat down together in the shade of a tree and told each other everything that had been happening in the two months since they parted. The Nicolsons' life at the out-station was a lonely one. They never set eyes on another soul apart from the black stock-rider who brought their stores on a couple of pack horses once a month.

'Aren't you scared?' Morag asked them.

The Nicolsons looked at each other in silence.

'Yes,' Kirsty admitted. 'Sometimes we're scared. There's nothing to see out there except the sky and the grass and the kangaroos and emus and snakes and all those birds. And the sheep! It's such a strange empty country, Morag! You're lucky, being here near the homestead with work to do in the house and other people to see. And Jimmy's here with you as well!'

'Not for much longer!' said Jimmy, laughing happily. 'The day after tomorrow I'm off! Mr Reekie heard from Captain Murray a few days ago, Kirsty, and he wants me back on his ship! He's given me a letter of safe-conduct to get me through any police patrols on the way so I'll be taking the track to Ballarat on my own two feet. Then I'll catch the horse-coach to Geelong. I've saved enough money for the fare. In a week from now I'll be safe and sound on the *Georgiana* again!'

'But you might come back, Jimmy,' said Morag wistfully. 'I heard you telling Mr Reekie that you might come back one day.'

'I might,' he said but he was still smiling at the thought of that beautiful white ship waiting for him in Corio Bay.

Donald MacDonald turned to the Nicolsons again.

'I hope you don't forget to read the Good Book, Alasdair, and to sing the Psalms every day. Just because it's a lonely life on your out-station, that doesn't mean you can forget about your Maker!'

'He never forgets!' said Shona Nicolson loyally. 'When I think back to that gravel pit where I lived with the three children for so long, I can hardly believe that I'm really here with a good man in a dry hut and with meat to eat three times a day! It seems like a dream!'

Everyone nodded.

'But I'd go back tomorrow if I had the chance!' said Morag's father.

'I'm never moving again!' said Effie. 'If you want to go back, Donald MacDonald, you'll go alone.'

'Don't you miss our little black house on Talisker, woman?' asked Donald sharply.

'I miss it, indeed, and I miss the dark Cuillins and the mists and the sea and my mother's green grave but nothing in the world would make me step onto another ship again. God has brought us here; now God can keep us here!'

Morag looked across at her mother in surprise. Effie MacDonald never usually said so much at once. She never used to sound so strong. This Colony seemed to be changing everyone in unexpected ways.

Late in the afternoon the Mathesons walked in from *Pittencairn*. They'd had to travel the twelve miles slowly to keep pace with Janet who couldn't move as spryly as she used to do. Morag thought Janet seemed smaller, somehow, and frailer, but Alec was as quick as ever on his limping leg and he had the fiddle still under his arm. In his other arm was some bulky package, well-wrapped up in a folded plaid.

'We'll be singing the old songs round our fire at the ceilidh tonight, Morag,' he said to her quietly with a wink. 'And maybe there'll be some dancing too. And we'll all have a good dram to drink. Mr Adams gave us a whole bottle of whisky just as we were setting off. He said he was so thankful we'd worked over Christmas that he wanted to give us something for New Year. His other shepherds were drunk for days on end at Christmas!'

'Whatever happened to the sheep?' asked Morag.

'Mr Adams and his overseer had to ride from one out-station to the next, making sure the flocks got some grass and water. He didn't have much of a Christmas himself. He said he was glad the folk from Skye don't bother about Christmas.'

'Mr Martin's given Father a bottle of whisky too,' said Morag. 'I think you're all going to be just as drunk as Mr Adams' shepherds were at Christmas!'

'No, no! I don't want to get really drunk or I couldn't fiddle and sing, could I? But I'll tell you what, Morag. I'd like to give your good father just a wee dram too much by the fire tonight. Not to make him dead drunk, of course. Just enough to make him drowsy and happy so he won't notice what we're up to. You see, I've got a fine idea for an old New Year's game the lads can do when midnight comes but it'd be best if your father slept through the whole thing. I wouldn't be wanting to distress the dear man at all. Do you think you could help me?'

'Easily!' said Morag. 'I'll sit next to him and I'll fill up his pannikin now and then when he's not looking. He's a sober man most of the year but New Year's different.'

'Good girl! Now you run off and tell that big brother of yours and Jimmy and the Nicolson boys that I want a word with them.'

'Can't I be in it too? And Kirsty?'

'No, it's the lads that must do it. That was always the way in the old days on Skye when I was young. The only sad thing is there'll be no dark man to come knocking on the door to bring us good luck. There always used to be some black-haired cousin to come visiting us at New Year on Skye.'

'There's my friend Kal-Kal!' said Morag excitedly. 'Would she do? I'm sure she'll want to come to the ceilidh anyway. She loves all our songs and stories.'

'She'd be better than no one, Morag, but it should really be a dark *man* not a wee black lassie. I'm not sure that the good luck ever comes with a lassie. Still, in a new country like this things might be different.'

'Where's Janet?' asked Morag, suddenly remembering. 'There's something I wanted to ask her.'

'She'll be baking fresh bread in the hut with your mother,' he said. 'Or she'll be resting under some old tree. She spends much more time just sitting these days than she ever used to. It's this heat that tires her out, I suppose.' Alec's voice sounded worried.

Janet wasn't in the hut with the other women. She'd wandered off by herself and was propped against the white trunk of a red-gum near the creek, gazing absently up into the sky. Morag ran to sit beside her, brushing off the ants that ran over her legs and hands. She told Janet straight away about the four mysterious Highlanders walking between the trees on the far side of the creek. Janet listened in silence.

'With a long box on their shoulders you say, Morag?' she said at last. 'Did it seem very heavy? Did they stagger under the weight of that box?'

'Oh no, Janet! It seemed as light as a feather. They walked along so easily, as if they never felt the weight of it at all.'

'Mmm. I'm not surprised. I thought the time must be coming soon.'

'What time, Janet? What do you mean?'

'It's best if I'm not saying too much, Morag my little one. You mustn't be worried at all about what you saw through the trees. When it comes to pass, then you'll understand. I daresay you'll be sad on that day and you'll shed some bitter tears. But *I'm* not sad! I'm happy! You really *do* have the Sight, just as I guessed. The Sight'll bring you many tears in a long lifetime, Morag, but it's a wonderful gift all the same. Just put the whole thing out of your mind for tonight.'

'I'll try,' said Morag. At that moment she smelt the camp-fire burning up in its ring of stones by a young wattle tree, not far from the hut.

'Come on, Janet!' she said.

The three families were soon sitting in a wide circle around the fire. The billy was boiling and the tea was made. Bread and cheese were passed from hand to hand. The two large whisky bottles began to circulate, the men drinking deep, the women taking a sip, the children passing it on. Morag sat close to her father and when he wasn't looking she topped up his pannikin with yet another generous measure of whisky. Kal-Kal was on Morag's other side, her eyes shining as she watched the glowing faces around the fire. Little Katie moved closer to Kal-Kal and smiled up at her. Allan sat near Kirsty.

Alec struck up an old tune. That was the signal for the stories to begin and Janet told the first as she always loved to do. She may have shrunk a little and grown frailer in these past two months, Morag thought to herself, but she still told the old tale of the water-horse from the Talisker River with as much vigour as ever. Then story followed story and song followed song. Morag sang again about the child of the swan; Effie sang about the cows on the shieling; Shona Nicolson sang the odd English song about the baby in the tree; Allan played slow sad tunes on his chanter. Kal-Kal sang a song in her own language about two strange animals called the bandicoot and the wombat.

Donald MacDonald was very sleepy but not so sleepy that he couldn't tell his own story again about the two brothers and the witch-cat. When he had finished he murmured softly, 'Of course, not a word of it's true, you know!' and with that he lay back on the earth and closed his eyes.

'Right!' cried Alec Matheson, leaping to his feet. 'Come on you lads! It must be almost midnight, judging by those stars up there. It's time for the old game!'

Morag couldn't help feeling envious as Allan and Jimmy, Ewen and Calum, Alasdair Nicolson and Tomas Matheson all left the fire and ran with excited laughter after Alec. Whatever they were up to, she wished she could do it too!

'I brought you a present,' whispered Kal-Kal in her ear. 'I heard your mother say that you used to give presents on Skye at the New Year.'

'So we did. But there's nothing much to give here. What have you brought me?'

'This!' said Kal-Kal. 'I made it myself!'

She held out something soft and brown. Morag couldn't quite see it in the firelight.

'What is it?' she asked, taking it in both hands and feeling the softness.

'It's a necklet of emu feathers! I gathered them myself and I sewed them onto that strip of possum skin. You put it round your neck and all those lovely feathers lie flat. Look, I'll tie it on for you.'

Morag bent her head and Kal-Kal slipped the necklet under her chin and tied it firmly at the back. The feathers, each one touching the next, brown at the stem where they were stitched to the band and paler at the tip, lay softly around her neck.

'It's lovely!' said Morag, touching the feathers with her fingers and trying desperately to think of something she could give to Kal-Kal in return. Suddenly she remembered. She slid her hand into the pocket of her skirt.

'Here's a present for you too!' she said, holding out the shell. 'It comes from the sea by the Isle of Skye!'

'From the sea!' breathed Kal-Kal as she took the white shell. 'Thank you, Morag! Look, I could bore a little hole in it just here and I could thread a string of grass through the hole and make a necklet for myself!'

'You could,' said Morag, surprised by such an idea but liking it all the same.

Kal-Kal sniffed at the shell.

'I can smell the sea!' she cried. 'I can smell the sea!'

At that very moment a fearful noise came from the trees beyond the hut. Kal-Kal clutched at Morag in terror.

'What is it?' she gasped.

'Just some old game for the New Year. Don't be scared.'

But as she saw the strange procession coming out of the bush and making for the circle around the fire, Morag felt pretty scared herself.

First came someone draped with the stiff dried hide of a cow. On his head was the cow's head. Two long fierce horns curled upwards and outwards. Behind this ghastly figure ran all the men and boys, shouting and bellowing.

Each one of them had a stick in his hand and as they ran they beat on the cow skin. It was like the terrible beat of a drum. Like the beat of many drums.

Kal-Kal shrieked in delight now. Her fears had gone.

The dark figures moved three times around the fire from east to west, sunwise, shouting, beating, laughing as they went. Then they ran three times around the hut, still beating, to drive the bad spirits away for the coming year. Then the limping man under the cow's head bent down to the fire. He dipped one edge of the hide into the flames and let it burn a little. A horrible stench filled the air.

'Sniff out the old year!' shouted Alec Matheson, peering out from the fearsome head of the cow. 'Sniff out the old year and sniff in the new! Sniff out the evil and sniff in the good!'

He ran around the circle from one person to the next, holding the smouldering corner of hide right up close to everyone's nose and telling them to smell it if they wanted good luck. They all sniffed obediently, shuddering at the acrid smell and laughing and pushing Alec on to the next person. All except Donald MacDonald. Donald lay deep asleep in a drunken daze, quite unaware of the antics going on around him. Just as well, thought Morag smiling to herself! She wondered how he could sleep through that terrible racket but sleep he did.

'Coo-ee! Coo-ee!'

A faint voice was calling from far beyond the homestead. The shrill cry came wavering out of the night. Everyone froze.

'Who is it?' asked Effie, startled.

No one knew.

'It might be your father, Kal-Kal,' said Morag. 'Trying to give us a fright.'

'That's not my father's voice. It's a white man.'

'We'd better wake Donald,' said Alec Matheson, his face

suddenly pale in the firelight. 'Just give me a minute to put this head and hide away. He mustn't see them!'

Effie shook Donald awake as Alec ran off. She threw a pannikin of cold water right into his face. He sat up and sniffed the air.

'What's that terrible smell, Effie?' he demanded.

Before she had time to open her mouth, the cry from the bush came again, closer this time.

'Coo-ee! Coo-ee!'

'Who's that?' asked Donald, looking around at the still faces.

'We don't know,' said Morag.

'Why don't you answer him?' asked Kal-Kal. 'It's probably just someone lost on the track.' And before anyone could stop her she answered the call herself, standing up and shouting back into the night.

'Coo-ee! Coo-ee!'

Her voice gave courage to Morag and the others. They all called together now, their eyes scanning the darkness.

'Coo-ee! Coo-ee!'

The stranger came closer and closer, guided by the fire and the chorus of voices. Fear was gripping Morag's stomach.

A tall thin figure came stumbling out of the bush. He staggered exhausted towards them.

'Donald MacDonald from Talisker!' he called, his voice breaking. 'Are you there?'

'Yes! I'm here!' cried Donald, suddenly shocked and sober. He leapt to his feet and stared. 'Who are you? Show your face, man!'

The tall figure fell headlong towards the ground. Donald caught him up in his arms and turned him to the fire. Now they could all see the face. It was not the face of a man at all but a boy of fifteen. His hair was black. His skin was deathly white. It was Rory MacRae!

'Rory!' gasped Morag.

Donald laid Rory on the ground and lifted up the boy's head. He held a pannikin of water to his lips. The dark eyes opened and looked around at the bewildering blur of familiar faces. He saw Morag and he smiled as he sipped the drink.

'How did you get here?' asked Morag, coming closer.

'Walked!' croaked Rory. 'Walked from Geelong to Ballarat and then out here. I got lost. I wasn't sure of the track. Then I saw the fire.'

'But where's your father? And did you find your mother?' Morag persisted, sitting on the ground beside him.

'We found her in Hobart Town,' he stammered. 'And we found the little ones, safe and sound. They've grown so much. They're not little any more!'

Rory stopped. Everyone waited.

'Well?' asked Morag.

'My mother ... my mother ...! I don't know how to tell you, Morag! She ... she's found a new husband in Hobart Town! She didn't think my father would ever follow her all the way out there so she married one of the convicts. He's a good kind man, she says, and she won't leave him. She told my father she never wanted to see his face again.'

Donald's voice was shocked.

'She has *two* husbands!'

Rory nodded.

'Most of the convicts get married,' he said. 'No one ever asks if they're married already.'

'She did the right thing!' said Effie. 'Your father's a hard man, Rory. She's better off without him!'

'Effie! Effie! What a terrible thing to say!' cried Donald.

'She's right,' said Rory. 'I told her so and then I left. I ran off before my father could stop me. I crossed Bass Strait by working on a ship and then I took to the track to find you all. I'm never going back to my father!'

Donald still shook his head but Morag burst in before he could say another word of rebuke.

'You've come just at the right time, Rory! Jimmy has to leave for his ship tomorrow. Mr Reekie'll be needing another worker.'

'And you've brought us all good luck!' cried Allan. 'Good luck for the New Year! A dark-haired boy! We were hoping you'd come, Rory!'

Everyone cheered.

'I do hope you'll stay here,' said Morag.

'I'll stay all right!' said Rory quietly. 'But Morag, do you know what I really want? In about five years' time when I've saved enough money? I want to buy a little piece of land of my own. Can you understand that?'

Morag nodded and smiled at Rory. She understood.

'Now let's dance!' cried Alec Matheson, drawing his bow across the strings.

'First a Psalm,' said Donald, 'and then the dancing.' He sang out the first line of the 40th Psalm.

Dh'fheith mi le foighid mhaith ri Dia

Even Rory managed to join in as they all took up the tune. Kal-Kal sang with them. She knew just how to do this strange wild singing now.

> *I waited for the Lord my God,*
> *And patiently did bear;*
> *At length to me he did incline*
> *My voice and cry to hear.*
>
> *He took me from a fearful pit,*
> *And from the miry clay,*
> *And on a rock he set my feet,*
> *Establishing my way.*

He put a new song in my mouth,
Our God to magnify:
Many shall see it, and shall fear,
And on the Lord rely.

Straight after the Psalm came the dancing. In pairs and in fours they danced around the dying fire till the night had ended. The sun was well risen by the time the families from Skye were ready to roll themselves up in their blankets and lie down under the trees. Far above their heads a wedge-tailed eagle soared into a blue sky, circling and circling, higher and higher. As Morag drifted off to sleep she could hear one lone voice still singing. It was Alec Matheson with his old song again.

May the fairies be with us wherever we go,
Over the green hills and over the sea,
Bringing us blessing so far from our home,
Over the green hills and over the sea.

WOLF

Gillian Cross

Cassy has never understood the connection between the secret midnight visitor to her nan's flat and her sudden trips to stay with her mother. But this time it seems different. She finds her mother living in a squat with her boyfriend Lyall and his son Robert. Lyall has devised a theatrical event for children on wolves, and Cassy is soon deeply involved in presenting it. Perhaps too involved – for she begins to sense a very real and terrifying wolf stalking her.

THE OUTSIDE CHILD

Nina Bawden

Imagine suddenly discovering you have a step-brother and -sister no one has ever told you about! It's the most exciting thing that's ever happened to Jane, and she can't wait to meet them. Perhaps at last she will become part of a 'proper' family, instead of for ever being the outside child. So begins a long search for her brother and sister, but when she finally does track them down, Jane finds there are still more surprises in store!

READ MORE IN PUFFIN

For children of all ages, Puffin represents quality and variety – the very best in publishing today around the world.

For complete information about books available from Puffin – and Penguin – and how to order them, contact us at the appropriate address below. Please note that for copyright reasons the selection of books varies from country to country.

On the worldwide web: www.penguin.co.uk

In the United Kingdom: Please write to *Dept. EP, Penguin Books Ltd, Bath Road, Harmondsworth, West Drayton, Middlesex UB7 ODA.*

In the United States: Please write to *Penguin Putnam inc., P.O. Box 12289, Dept B, Newark, New Jersey 07101-5289* or call 1-800-788-6262

In Canada: Please write to *Penguin Books Canada Ltd, 10 Alcorn Avenue, Suite 300, Toronto, Ontario M4V 3B2*

In Australia: Please write to *Penguin Books Australia Ltd, P.O. Box 257, Ringwood, Victoria 3134*

In New Zealand: Please write to *Penguin Books (NZ) Ltd, Private Bag 102902, North Shore Mail Centre, Auckland 10*

In India: Please write to *Penguin Books India Pvt Ltd, 11 Panscheel Shopping Centre, Panscheel Park, New Delhi 110 017*

In the Netherlands: Please write to *Penguin Books Netherlands bv, Postbus 3507, NL-1001 AH Amsterdam*

In Germany: Please write to *Penguin Books Deutschland GmbH, Metzlerstrasse 26, 60594 Frankfurt am Main*

In Spain: Please write to *Penguin Books S. A., Bravo Murillo 19, 1° B, 28015 Madrid*

In Italy: Please write to *Penguin Italia s.r.l., Via Felice Casati 20, I-20124 Milano*

In France: Please write to *Penguin France S. A., 17 rue Lejeune, F-31000 Toulouse*

In Japan: Please write to *Penguin Books Japan, Ishikiribashi Building, 2-5-4, Suido, Bunkyo-ku, Tokyo 112*

In South Africa: Please write to *Longman Penguin Southern Africa (Pty) Ltd, Private Bag X08, Bertsham 2013*